Nurse Claire Baxter jumps at the chance of a year in Paris looking after the delicate five-year-old nephew of the brilliant heart surgeon André Dubois. But the job proves quite a challenge, especially as the high-handed surgeon has apparently already driven away one English nurse!

Books you will enjoy in our Doctor–Nurse series:

SHAMROCK NURSE by Elspeth O'Brien
ICE VENTURE NURSE by Lydia Balmain
TREAD SOFTLY, NURSE by Lynne Collins
DR VENABLES' PRACTICE by Anne Vinton
NURSE OVERBOARD by Meg Wisgate
EMERGENCY NURSE by Grace Read
DOCTORS IN DISPUTE by Jean Evans
WRONG DOCTOR JOHN by Kate Starr
AUSTRIAN INTERLUDE by Lee Stafford
SECOND CHANCE AT LOVE by Zara Holman
TRIO OF DOCTORS by Lindsay Hicks
CASSANDRA BY CHANCE by Betty Neels
SURGEON IN DANGER by Kate Ashton
VENETIAN DOCTOR by Elspeth O'Brien
IN THE NAME OF LOVE by Hazel Fisher
DEAR DOCTOR MARCUS by Barbara Perkins
RAINBOW SUMMER by Sarah Franklin
SOLO SURGEON by Lynne Collins
NEW DOCTOR AT THE BORONIA by Lilian Darcy
HEALERS OF THE NIGHT by Anne Vinton
THE RETURN OF DR BORIS by Lisa Cooper
DOCTOR IN NEW GUINEA by Dana James
ROSES FOR CHRISTMAS by Betty Neels

PARIS NURSE

BY

MARGARET BARKER

MILLS & BOON LIMITED
London · Sydney · Toronto

First published in Great Britain 1983 by
Mills & Boon Limited, 15–16 Brook's Mews,
London W1A 1DR

ISBN 0 263 74506 6

Set in 11 on 12½ pt Linotron Times
03/1283

Photoset by Rowland Phototypesetting Ltd
Bury St Edmunds, Suffolk
Made and printed in Great Britain by
Richard Clay (The Chaucer Press) Ltd,
Bungay, Suffolk

CHAPTER ONE

CLAIRE was feeling decidedly pleased with herself. Far below the plane, she could see the blue waters of the English Channel, dotted here and there with tiny ships, shining in the sunlight. It was marvellous to get away from hospital life for a while. She enjoyed her work as a staff nurse in the cardiac unit of a London teaching hospital, but when the opportunity to spend a year in Paris had arisen, she had jumped at it.

'In some ways, it's a waste of your talents,' Dr Smithson had said to her. 'But you are the only person I could possibly recommend to such a brilliant heart surgeon as André Dubois. He has asked me to find someone who is experienced in cardiology and paediatrics, and who can speak French. You fit the bill admirably. André Dubois wants someone to look after his five-year-old nephew, who has a congenital heart defect, and his four-year-old niece.'

Claire gathered that she would be required to live with the family, and that her salary would be more than twice the amount she was now receiving. A year in Paris also meant that she would be able to see more of Robert Smith, who was teaching English out there. All in all, a wise move, she thought.

'We are beginning our descent to Paris,' said the voice over the intercom. 'Please fasten your seat belts, and extinguish your cigarettes.'

Claire could see French fields and woods, spread out below her like a patchwork quilt; a motorway, thronged with minute cars and lorries sliced through it, piercing the northern suburbs of Paris in the hazy distance, where tower blocks reached up towards the sky.

The plane flew gently down on to the tarmac and taxied along to a standstill. The official voice continued, 'Air France hopes you have enjoyed your flight and that we shall have the pleasure of your company again.'

The smiling stewardesses said goodbye as she left the plane and walked into the new Charles de Gaulle airport. She waited in the baggage-claim area, picked up her suitcase, and then went out through Customs. As she started to go through the airport doors, someone took hold of her arm and held her back. Turning round, she faced a tall, dark man, with a deeply sun-tanned but unsmiling face.

'I'm sorry if I startled you,' he said, in perfect English but with a slight French accent. 'I decided to collect you myself, so that I can brief you before we meet the family. I am André Dubois. I presume you are Claire Baxter. My good friend Mark Smithson described you to me, and you were the only person on the plane with long blonde hair and piercing blue eyes.'

His expression did not change as he said this. He

was merely making an observation. His eyes were cold, almost hostile, as he took her arm and steered her firmly along the pavement to a long, low sports car.

'Get in,' he commanded, unceremoniously.

Claire climbed in, not trusting herself to speak. He let in the clutch, expertly, and the car shot forward through the maze of vehicles which surrounded the airport. Soon they were hurtling along the road to Paris. He was an excellent driver, concentrating his whole attention on the road and the surrounding traffic, which pulled over into an inside lane as he impatiently hooted his horn and rushed past them. At last they came to Porte de la Chapelle, where the road from the airport joins the *périphérique*, the huge motorway which encircles Paris.

'I presume you do have a voice,' André Dubois shouted at her, above the roar of the traffic.

'Yes, of course,' answered Claire, feeling angry and humiliated, but not daring to voice her feelings to the great man himself.

'Why did you take this post?' he shouted at her.

She was startled by his abrupt manner.

'I felt it was a challenge,' she answered.

André Dubois threw back his head and laughed.

'You'll have to do better than that', he said. 'I suppose you like the salary.'

Claire started to reply, but he cut her short.

'No matter why you came. You were highly recommended for your professional competence.

Nothing else matters to me. You are to take care of my nephew, Philippe.'

'Would you explain what this entails,' ventured Claire, raising her voice to make sure she was heard.

'Good heavens, child, I can't give you a briefing here, on the *périphérique.* Wait until I can find a quiet spot.'

Claire was furious. Great man or not, he had no right to treat her like a schoolgirl. She sat silently, determined not to speak unless spoken to.

At Porte de la Muette, he turned his car off the *périphérique* into the Bois de Boulogne, and brought it to a halt by the lakeside. It was so peaceful after the noise of the traffic and the rush of the wind, that Claire leaned back and relaxed, drinking in the woodland scenery.

'Let's walk,' he said briefly, as he climbed out, slamming the door.

Claire struggled out of the low sports car, aware that André Dubois was watching her with an amused smile, but was not offering to help.

'We'll go over to the island,' he said imperiously. 'We can talk there.'

He set off at a quick pace, down the grassy bank towards the lake, and Claire hurried after him.

'Come on,' he shouted over his shoulder, without turning round. 'The ferry's about to go. Hurry up.'

The ferry-boat man had seen them coming, and he waited. André leapt into the boat and sat down.

Claire arrived several seconds later, and was relieved that the friendly ferryman helped her aboard. She sank down, panting, on the seat next to André.

'My, we are out of condition, aren't we!' he said. 'I thought you English girls were supposed to be fitness freaks. Don't you go jogging in the park in the morning?'

'I've never been able to find the time,' said Claire icily.

'Oh, but you must make the time to keep fit,' he continued. 'We can't have you falling ill on the job out here.'

Claire made no reply to this. She purposely fixed her eyes on the blue water. The boat was speeding across its surface, and she told herself to relax and enjoy it. She would nurse her patient as skilfully and efficiently as possible, and ignore the surgeon's unpleasant manner.

The boat reached the island and they walked across the landing stage to the restaurant. André Dubois motioned Claire towards an outside table which looked out on to the lake.

'What would you like to drink?' he asked as they sat down.

'Coffe would be nice,' said Claire.

'*Deux cafés,*' he said to the waiter, then frowning slightly, he turned back to Claire.

'I want you to realise that everything I say is in the strictest confidence.'

Claire nodded. 'Of course.'

'My nephew Philippe was born with a defective mitral valve, as you know. It was operated on when he was a baby, but he has always been delicate. I think his condition is worsening, and it may be necessary to operate again. Naturally, I'm holding out as long as possible. The older he is, the more chance there is of survival. I want you to watch him carefully, and report any significant symptoms of cardiac malfunctioning to me, at once—no matter what time of the day or night. Telephone me at the hospital or at my flat; here are the numbers.'

Claire wrote them in her diary. Numerous questions sprang to her mind, but she decided to wait until later.

'My sister is a career woman,' he continued. 'She has no interest in her children.'

Claire gasped in surprise.

'Does that shock you?' asked André Dubois.

'Perhaps you have over-stated the case,' ventured Claire.

'I should like to think so, but I'm afraid that wouldn't be true,' he said.

'I can believe that she is a career woman, but that she takes no interest in her children . . . well . . . that's quite unnatural for a mother,' said Claire.

'Perhaps I should explain,' he said. 'My sister, Hélène, was a successful dress designer when she married. Two years later her husband had a heart attack and died, leaving her with a large fortune, and two small children. She simply went back to her career to help her forget, and she paid to have the children looked after. In Simone's case this worked very well, but I have always had to supervise Philippe's nursing care. My sister simply refuses to believe that he is ill—delicate, yes, but ill, no.'

'What sort of nursing care has he had?' asked Claire, her interest in the case overcoming her dislike of the great heart specialist.

'In my opinion, it has been inadequate,' said André Dubois. 'I intervened last year, and appointed a cardiac nurse.' He paused, then continued. 'But it didn't work out,' he said quietly.

Claire glanced at him, but he gave no further reasons for the failure, and she decided it was better not to ask. She took a sip of the strong, black coffee before saying,

'Was she French?'

'No, she was English,' he said abruptly. 'My sister likes to have English nurses for her children, as she wants them to be bilingual. Our mother was American. Personally, I would have preferred to appoint one of the nurses from my own hospital.'

Claire looked out across the water towards the tree-clad shore of the opposite bank of the lake. The afternoon sun shone on the path which encircled the shore, where people were enjoying the warmth of its rays. An unending stream of joggers passed along the path; there were mothers with their children, and dog-lovers exercising their pets. Her mind took it all in, while at the same time she reviewed what she had just heard. This job was definitely going to be a challenge, and she would take it, in spite of the fact that her employer seemed to have taken such a dislike to her.

André Dubois paid the bill and stood up. To her surprise he took her arm and guided her towards the path by the water's edge.

'I want you to see how lovely my country is,' he was saying. 'It is important that you love France.'

'Oh, but I do,' said Claire honestly. 'I really do, otherwise I wouldn't have come.'

'Then it's not just professional interest that brings you here?' he asked. 'Tell me, do you have any friends in Paris?' He was smiling at her, not just with his lips, but with his eyes.

Claire thought quickly before answering, 'I have a boyfriend who teaches English here.'

The smile vanished from his face, and his eyes became cold.

'I see,' he said. 'I hope you will not allow your private life to interfere with your professional duties.'

'Of course not,' said Claire. 'Anyway, he's not very important to me. Just a boyfriend I've known for some time.'

'Just a boyfriend,' he repeated quietly. 'I suppose you have many boyfriends?'

'I think my private life is my own affair,' Claire said lightly.

'Of course,' he said coldly. 'But I hope you will keep it private.'

He turned abruptly and started to walk quickly along the path towards the ferry-boat. They crossed back to the mainland and were soon gliding down a tree-shaded avenue. He screeched to a halt inside the underground car park of an expensive apartment building. This time he opened the door of the car and helped her out. She looked at him quizzically as they stepped into the lift. He was standing much too close for comfort. She could smell his expensive after-shave, and found the experience unnerving. If only he weren't so arrogant, he would be so attractive, she thought.

They stepped out into the penthouse suite, which overlooked the Bois de Boulogne on one side and had a magnificent view up the tree-lined avenue towards the Arc de Triomphe on the other. Claire found it breathtakingly beautiful as she walked across the thick carpet towards the roof-top garden, where the family were waiting to greet her. Hélène Flament, a tall, strikingly elegant lady came to meet her with outstretched hands.

'Welcome, Nurse Baxter,' she said in English, then turning towards her brother, she embraced him. 'Thank you, André. It was good of you to come. I'm glad you were not too busy.'

'I can always find time to meet a pretty girl at the airport.' He smiled, then scooping up his little niece into his arms, he said to Claire, 'This is Simone.'

She was a vivacious little creature, full of life, in contrast to her brother, who hung back nervously. Simone leaned forward and kissed Claire on both cheeks.

'Come and meet Nurse Baxter,' said André, but

Philippe refused to move. Although one year older than his sister he was slightly smaller, and much thinner. Claire's heart went out to him at once.

'You will take tea with us?' said Hélène.

'I'd love to,' said Claire, settling herself into an armchair, amid the exotic roof-top plants. 'What a fabulous view you have up here. I suppose it compensates for living in a city.'

'Oh, but we don't live here all the time,' said Hélène. 'We have a house by the sea, where we spend as much time as possible. It's so good for the children—especially Philippe who is always so pale, poor little mite.'

André said he had no time for tea, as he had to get back to the hospital.

'But you will dine with us this evening, won't you?' said Hélène.

'If I can; it depends on how soon I can get away. Don't wait for me.'

He walked briskly out of the room, without looking at Claire.

'We always take tea in the afternoon,' Hélène said to Claire when André had gone. 'Just like you do in England. My mother was American. That's why I want them to be bilingual. Have you done any private nursing before?'

'No, I've been working with cardiac patients since I qualified as an SRN.'

'Ah yes, I suppose that's why my brother appointed you. He's obsessed by Philippe's heart condition,' she said languidly.

Claire glanced across at her and realised that she seemed to have no interest in the situation. She was calmly smoking a cigarette, and Claire noticed that Philippe had moved to the other end of the room so that the smoke would not reach him.

'He's always been a delicate child,' continued Hélène in a matter-of-fact voice. 'But the heart condition was put right when he was a baby. I think André just likes spoiling him. Still, I don't mind having extra help around, to ease the load.'

The children were beginning to quarrel, and Claire started to calm them down.

'I think the children are getting tired,' said Hélène. 'Let's take them down to the nursery, then I can show you where everything is kept. We do, of course, have a nursery-maid who looks after all the domestic arrangements, but I would like you to supervise their general welfare while I'm away.'

'Are you going away?' asked Claire, surprised.

'Yes, didn't André tell you? I thought he would have said something about it. I'm a dress designer, and my work often takes me away. Tomorrow I have to go to New York for a couple of weeks. It's fortunate that you arrived today. You will be in charge of the children, but the domestic staff are at your disposal.' Hélène rang a bell, and as if by magic, two maids appeared, one to clear the tea things, and one to take the children to the nursery.

'This is Marie, our nursery-maid,' said Hélène. 'We'll come down to the nursery with you, Marie. This is Nurse Baxter,' she said in French.

Marie smiled briefly at Claire as she gathered up the toys.

'Let me help you,' said Claire, picking up little Philippe and making her way through the roof garden.

The nursery suite was, as Claire expected, furnished in a most luxurious style, and no expense had been spared. She decided it was going to be an interesting experience, working in such a household. There were shelves full of expensive toys and educational books, written in both English and French. Certainly the children lacked nothing that money could buy. Hélène showed her round the suite; the children had their own bathroom, playroom, bedrooms, dining-room, and there was a bedroom and a kitchen for the maid.

'It's quite delightful,' said Claire enthusiastically, as she wandered from room to room.

'You must let me know if there's anything else you need here,' said Hélène. 'Anything at all. You have only to ask.' She smiled at Claire. 'Now we'll leave Marie to settle the children. Come and see if you like your own room. You must be feeling tired after your journey.'

She led Claire down a corridor and opened a door which led into a large, bright room with a balcony. Claire found it enchanting; she went out eagerly on to the balcony to admire the view of Paris.

'Do you like it?' asked Hélène.

'It's lovely,' said Claire.

'I'm glad you think so, because I do want you to stay with us. It's important for me to have peace of mind when I'm away from home. My work is extremely interesting, but very exacting. I couldn't carry on if I didn't think all was well at home.' She smiled at Claire. 'When you have finished unpacking, come to the drawing-room. We'll have an aperitif before dinner.' She moved across the room. 'I'll ring for a maid to help you unpack.'

'Oh, please don't,' said Claire hastily. 'I can manage by myself.'

'Very well. Take your time.' Hélène went out, closing the door softly behind her.

Claire breathed a sigh of happiness; everything seemed to be working out beautifully, apart from the supercilious André Dubois. Crossing the room, she went into her bathroom and revelled in a long, luxurious bath, sprinkled liberally with the expensive bath-foam which she had found on the edge of the bath. Then, after unpacking, she carefully chose her dress for the evening. It was in cream linen, a simple, classic style, which showed off her slim figure to perfection. She dressed slowly, then went out into the corridor in search of the drawing-room. There seemed to be endless doors: it was like a hotel from which all possible signs and indications had been removed. She walked from one end of the corridor and back again, but there seemed to be no way out. Just as she was about to despair, she noticed she had passed the lift.

Perhaps I can retrace my steps from there, she thought.

She walked over, turned her back to it, and looked in the direction of the roof garden. At that moment, the lift doors opened and someone stepped out, almost knocking her over. She felt strong arms holding her round the waist, preventing her from falling.

'What a stupid place to stand,' said a deep, manly voice behind her. She turned round as André released his grip. The brief touch of his hands had sent shivers down her spine.

'Actually, I was trying to find my way to the drawing-room,' Claire said coldly.

'Then allow me to escort you,' he smiled, with instant composure. It was a brittle smile, and his eyes remained cold and unsympathetic.

They went along the corridor together, and André opened the door to the drawing-room. The windows were wide open on to a balcony, where Hélène was enjoying the warm summer evening.

'Come out here for a drink,' she called.

They joined her outside, and André asked Claire what she would like. She glanced anxiously at the drinks tray, to see if there was anything she recognised.

'Whatever you prefer, I'm sure we can find it for you,' said Hélène helpfully. 'Or would you like to try my favourite drink – kir?'

'What's that?' asked Claire.

'It's *crème de cassis* with white wine.'

Claire looked at Hélène's dark, rose-coloured drink. 'It sounds delightful,' she said. 'Yes please.'

She found she had made a good choice, and the warmth of the evening sun, coupled with the mellowing effect of the drink helped to ease away the tension she felt whenever she was close to André.

'Paris is so beautiful at this time of the year,' he was saying. 'Before it gets too hot and crowded with tourists. We always go away to our house at Arcachon when Paris becomes unbearable.'

'I've been thinking,' said Hélène. 'Why don't we send Nurse Baxter and the children to the house while I'm in New York? It would be so good for them.'

André looked annoyed. 'I don't think that's a good idea at all,' he snapped. 'I should prefer to keep an eye on the children while you are away.'

'Oh don't be silly,' said Hélène. 'Nurse Baxter is perfectly capable of looking after them, and she will have Madame Thiret to help her.'

'Who is Madame Thiret?' asked Claire, hoping that perhaps she could have some say in the matter.

'She's the old housekeeper who brought me up,' André answered, his voice becoming warmer as he spoke about Madame Thiret. 'Yes, I suppose you might be all right at the house,' he conceded uncertainly, looking sternly at Claire.

Claire returned his gaze coldly. 'Quite frankly I would prefer to stay in Paris,' she said evenly, 'but if Madame Flament would like the children to go to the sea, I will take them.'

Hélène was startled at the obvious hostility between Claire and her brother; it was probably a good idea to keep them apart, she thought.

'I'm sure you will enjoy your stay at Arcachon,' she said. 'I'll phone Madame Thiret tonight and tell her you're coming.'

She rang a bell and a maid appeared.

'We're ready for dinner now,' she said.

CHAPTER TWO

DINNER was a long, complicated affair, and Claire found it something of a strain to eat so many courses. The ice-cold melon was already set at the table, and André Dubois served a chilled sweet white wine to drink with it. Although he was seated next to Claire, he paid her little attention, for he mostly carried on a voluble conversation in rapid French with his sister. The trout which followed was cooked in white wine and mushrooms, served with a cream sauce, and Claire found herself engrossed in the enjoyable task of stripping the delicious fish from the bones. She also helped herself to the crisp French bread and salty butter on the table, and by the end of the course found she had no more appetite.

After a flurry of conversation, André announced that they were now going to have *gigot d'agneau*, which turned out to be a very rare leg of lamb. Even had she been hungry Claire doubted if she could have eaten much of the bright red meat; in addition it had been spiked with garlic, which she did not like. She ate very little, and was relieved when she could clear her plate for the *salade*. This was a crisp lettuce, served with a French dressing, and although Claire found it unusual to eat lettuce by itself, after the meat course it proved to be most refreshing, and somehow rekindled her appetite, so that she was able to eat a little cheese, and then a lemon sorbet.

At the end of the meal, Claire said she would like to go and look at her patient. Hélène seemed slightly amused at this. 'I don't think it's necessary, my dear. Marie is quite capable of putting the children to bed.'

'I should like to check on Philippe's condition,' said Claire quietly. 'After all, that's what I'm here for.'

'Yes, of course,' André smiled at her, and this time there was a warmth in his smile. 'Nurse Baxter is quite right.'

Claire rose from the table, and went towards the door.

'You will come back for coffee, I hope,' said Hélène.

'Thank you, I will.'

As the door closed behind Claire, she heard Hélène saying,

'Quite a little Florence Nightingale you've found, André. I hope we shan't have any complications this time.'

She was speaking quickly and quietly in French, presuming that Claire would not hear her. Claire began to wonder about the English nurse who had been here last year. Perhaps she had found the situation unpleasant. Oh well, whatever it was, she was not going to be beaten.

She walked along to the nursery suite. Marie was

sitting outside Philippe's room, and she smiled as Claire approached.

'He's sleeping peacefully,' she said in French.

'I'll just go in and see him,' said Claire.

She went quietly into the little boy's room and bent over his bed. The soft, even breathing assured her that all was well for the moment. She took his pulse, and was alarmed at the irregularity.

'Call me if there's any change in his condition,' she said to Marie as she went out. Marie smiled and nodded.

She walked resolutely back to the drawing room, feeling her professional interest roused by this small scrap of a boy. Her presence in this household was absolutely essential, and she determined to keep personal prejudices at bay. André Dubois' dislike of her, and his high-handed manner were not going to prevent her from doing a good job.

She opened the drawing-room door and went in. André and Hélène were drinking coffee. She spoke quickly and quietly to André, 'Would you check on Philippe's condition before you go. I'm a little worried about the irregularity of his pulse.'

'Of course I will. I was going to anyway, but thank you for the information.'

'Come and have some coffee,' said Hélène.

A maid poured coffee from a silver coffee-pot, and brought it over to Claire; she began to relax again. She seemed to have got through her first evening without too many problems. Just as she was beginning to congratulate herself, a maid entered.

'*Excusez-moi*, mademoiselle,' she said to Claire. '*Téléphone pour vous.*'

'For me?' asked Claire, in surprise.

'I expect it's your English boyfriend,' said André drily. 'I would have thought he could have left you alone on your first evening.'

'André!' said Hélène. 'Nurse Baxter has a right to her own private life. There is a phone in the next room, Nurse Baxter.'

Claire hurried out and picked up the phone.

'Robert!' she said. 'I didn't expect to hear from you so soon. Where are you?'

'Downstairs in the entrance hall. I couldn't wait to see you,' the familiar voice said. 'Can you get away now?'

'Not really, I've only arrived in Paris today, and I have to prepare for a trip to Arcachon. Besides, I'm worried about my patient. I'd like to stay near him tonight.'

'Oh, come off it, Claire. They managed without you until now. The break will do you good. You've got to have some time off-duty you know.'

'I'll come out for a short while,' Claire said. 'But not too long. I'll have to check with my employer first. Wait for me in the hall.'

'Good girl. Don't be long.'

Claire went back into the drawing-room. The atmosphere was charged with electricity. Hélène had obviously been having words with her brother, but she smiled at Claire when she came in.

'Do you mind if I go out for a short while?' asked Claire.

'Of course not, my dear,' said Hélène. 'I'm so glad you have friends here in Paris.'

'She has a boyfriend,' said André coldly. 'Personally, I don't think it advisable for a young girl to go out alone with a man, at this time of night.'

'Oh, come now, André,' said Hélène. 'This is obviously a friend she has known for some time, isn't that so, Nurse Baxter?'

'Yes, of course. I've known Robert for several years. Besides which, I'm not a young girl.' She turned towards André. 'I'm twenty-four years old.'

He laughed. '*Bien sûr, très vieille*, positively ancient. Run along with you. It never surprises me what you English girls get up to.' He turned abruptly and went out on to the balcony.

Claire took a deep breath, and followed him out. He looked at her with an arrogant, hostile stare.

'I really am concerned about Philippe's condition,' she said quietly.

'Of course you are.' His eyes softened as he looked down on her. 'Don't worry, I'll keep a check on him until you get back—but don't be late. I have to be in theatre early tomorrow.'

'I won't be late,' promised Claire.

Downstairs in the hall, Robert was becoming impatient. He came rushing across to meet her, his fair, curly hair falling nonchalantly over his eyes.

He threw his arms round her and clasped her warmly.

'It's good to see you, Claire. I was delighted when I got your letter. Fancy you here in Paris! It's too good to be true.'

They went out into the warm night, up the avenue to the Arc de Triomphe, and were soon walking down the Champs-Elysées. The bright lights of the showrooms, cinemas and restaurants, together with the incessant traffic and crowds of pedestrians made it a hive of activity. People sat at tables, both in the restaurants and also outside on the pavement, drinking, eating, talking, smoking, or simply idling away the summer evening. Robert found a table for them outside one of the cafés, and ordered coffee and cognac. He reached across the table and took her hand.

'I never thought you'd come out here to see me,' he said, his bright eyes shining happily.

Claire was somewhat taken aback.

'I didn't exactly come out here to see you, Robert,' she said gently, as she sipped the strong coffee. 'I do have a job here, you know.'

'Yes, but you must have wanted to come to Paris,' he insisted.

'Of course I wanted to come to Paris. That's what I'm trying to tell you—oh, never mind,' she finished, lamely. 'Let's not spoil it . . . Isn't it beautiful here . . . I keep pinching myself to make sure I'm awake.'

'We're going to have a marvellous time

together,' continued Robert. 'When do you go off to Arcachon?'

'Tomorrow, I think,' said Claire quickly.

'Tomorrow!' echoed Robert.

'Yes, but only for a couple of weeks.'

'OK, I'll see you when you get back.' He seemed to accept the situation. 'Meanwhile, there's tonight. We must make the most of it. Come back to my flat, Claire.'

Claire was alarmed at the urgency in his voice.

'Robert, it's getting late; I've a busy day ahead of me, and anyway, I've got to get back to my patient.'

'So you said,' he muttered. 'It seems unreasonable of them to expect you to work so late. Haven't they got a relief nurse?'

'It's all rather complicated . . .' began Claire.

'So it would seem,' he said impatiently. 'Oh, well, let's go for a short walk along the river, then. Just for a few minutes—they can't object to that.'

Robert took her arm and steered her down the Champs-Elysées, where the constant traffic hurtled furiously past as if it were the middle of the day, through the gardens of the Grand Palais, and down to the river. They crossed to the Left Bank, and stood gazing into the Seine, which was lit by the lights from both sides, and by the illuminated boats which skimmed through it. Further down the river, Claire could see the Eiffel Tower, gleaming majestically in the moonlight.

'It's all so beautiful,' murmured Claire. Robert took her hand, and guided her along the riverside path. Suddenly she remembered her promise to André.

'I have to go back now,' she said, turning quickly, but Robert laid a restraining hand on her arm, and spun her round to face him.

'Not yet, please,' he implored, and before she could stop him, he had taken her in his arms. His mouth hungrily sought hers, parting her lips brutally, with unexpected pressure. Claire pulled herself away from him.

'No, Robert, I must go,' she insisted.

He laughed, huskily. 'You come all this way to see me, and I'm not even allowed a goodnight kiss.'

'Robert, you don't understand; I didn't come all this way just to see you. We've always been good friends—nothing more. Please take me back now.'

He gave a resigned shrug, and escorted her to the nearby Metro station. He already had some tickets, so they were quickly through the automatic barriers and on to a train. With only one change they were soon back at the Arc de Triomphe, where they silently retraced their steps, until they reached the entrance hall of the apartment building. Impulsively she reached up and kissed his cheek; surprised, he bent towards her, to prolong the contact, but she evaded his grasp, as she skipped quickly towards the lift.

'I'll ring you when I get back,' she called, as the lift doors closed. Why was her heart pounding as the lift went upwards towards the penthouse suite? It had nothing to do with her brief encounter with

Robert. She felt only too glad to escape, so what was this unbearable feeling of anticipation?

The lift stopped at the top floor, and she walked out into the corridor. The apartment was apparently deserted. Low lights cast a sombre glow from the roof garden, but everywhere else was in darkness. Claire glanced at her watch, and was alarmed to see it was almost midnight. A rustling among the plants told her that she was not alone; the tall figure of André Dubois came towards her. His eyes pierced inside her as he spoke, angrily.

'So you expected me to wait all night for you . . . I didn't know whether you would return at all. I know so little of the customs of your country,' he said mockingly. 'But I see you enjoyed yourself.'

He took a linen handkerchief from his pocket, and deliberately wiped away a smear of lipstick which had spread across her cheek. 'Did you go back to his apartment, or did you make love by the river?'

'I don't have to answer your personal questions,' said Claire quietly. 'How is my patient?'

'Ah, so now you are concerned about your patient. How very gratifying. Fortunately your patient's condition is satisfactory. Marie will waken you if there is any change. You may go to bed now.'

Claire walked down the corridor towards her room, aware that André was accompanying her, but deliberately keeping a wide space between them. He opened her bedroom door, then stood back to let her pass through. As she went in he took her hand and pressed it lightly to his lips.

'*Bonsoir, chérie*,' he said softly, smiling gently down at her. '*Dormez bien*.'

Claire turned, surprised at the change in his manner, but he had already released her hand, and was striding purposefully away. Her thoughts were in turmoil as she closed the door and leaned against it. She was exhausted, but it was a long time before she could fall asleep.

Next morning, however, she awoke refreshed, and ready to take whatever the day presented. She found Hélène having breakfast with the children in the nursery suite.

'Good morning,' said Hélène. 'Did you sleep well?'

'Yes, thank you.' Claire sat down at the table, and Hélène passed her a croissant.

'*Café au lait*?' said Hélène, and Claire nodded, as she savoured the delicious flaky pastry of the croissant.

'How was the date with the boyfriend?' Hélène was smiling at her. Claire smiled back.

'Fine. We walked by the river, and admired the lights of Paris.'

'Yes, it really is beautiful at night. But you'll love Arcachon,' continued Hélène. 'I've arranged for our chauffeur to drive you down in the car. He can stay with you, and bring you back in two weeks. I said you would be ready about ten. Does that give you enough time?'

'Yes, of course. I'd like to spend some time with Philippe before we go, just to see that he's fit to travel.'

'Oh, that won't be necessary—André called in on his way to the hospital and checked him over. He was quite satisfied.' Hélène stood up. 'I must be off to catch my plane.'

The children went to kiss their mother, but they were obviously used to being left behind, and did not make a fuss when Hélène left the room. Marie arrived to say that the children's cases were packed, so Claire left the children with her and went off to prepare her own things.

They left promptly at ten, Claire sitting in the back of the large, comfortable limousine, with the children. Henri, the chauffeur, drove speedily out of Paris on to the motorway, and soon they were heading south. It was a hot day and Claire was glad of the air-conditioning in the car. She amused the children until they became tired and fell asleep, leaning against her, one on either side. The countryside changed gradually, becoming softer and more open.

At lunchtime, Claire gently woke the children. Henri had pulled the car into the car-park of a delighful country restaurant near Poitiers, where he assured her the family always dined on their way to Arcachon. The head waiter came to greet them, and ushered them to a table overlooking a cool courtyard.

The lunch was excellent, and Claire was pleased

with the way Philippe and Simone behaved at table. She found they were beginning to understand much of what she said to them in English, and Simone even tried to say a few phrases which her mother had taught her. After lunch they continued their journey, down the new motorway to Bordeaux, then out to the coast at Arcachon.

It was a beautiful old house, on the outskirts of the town, with a private beach and a large garden. The children, glad to be out of the car, ran amongst the shady trees as soon as they were released. Claire followed them, while the chauffeur carried the luggage into the house. The garden stretched down to the beach, and was ideal for the children. Claire felt immediately that she was going to enjoy herself there. Suddenly she heard a voice calling from the house. Turning, she saw a tall, imperious old lady standing on the front steps. Claire took hold of the children, and went to meet her. The old lady bent forward and held out her hand.

'*Bonjour* mademoiselle; *je suis* Madame Thiret,' she said. '*Parlez-vous français?*'

'*Oui* madame,' said Claire quickly, and the conversation continued in French.

'Then why were you speaking English to the children just now?' the old lady asked sharply.

'Their mother wants them to learn English,' said Claire defensively.

'Does she indeed,' retorted Madame Thiret. 'But then I suppose she would. What does Monsieur André think?'

'About what?' asked Claire.

'About the children speaking English, of course,' Madame Thiret said sharply.

'I think he approves,' said Claire quietly. Madame Thiret did not reply. She turned and went into the house.

'Follow me, Nurse,' she said coldly.

Claire followed Madame Thiret into the house, and up a winding staircase.

'This will be your room,' the old lady said, pausing in front of a cream-coloured door. She turned and started to go down the stairs.

'Where are the children going to sleep?' asked Claire.

'They will have the room next to mine, as their uncle did when he was a boy,' was the haughty reply.

Claire decided that this would have to be changed, but that now was not the time to start arguing. How could she possibly keep an eye on Philippe if he was over in the other side of the house? She would have to ring André and ask him to intervene.

The atmosphere at dinner was extremely strained. Madame Thiret sat at the head of the table and served out large helpings which the children could not possibly eat, then scolded them for leaving food on their plates. Simone started to speak English to Claire, but the old housekeeper immediately stopped her.

'We will speak French here,' she said sternly.

When the meal ended, Madame Thiret said she was going to put the children to bed.

'I'll come with you,' said Claire.

'There's no need,' said the old lady coldly. 'I've been caring for this family since before you were born, child. You can take them to the beach in the morning.'

This was too much. Claire took a deep breath before she spoke. 'Madame, I should like to make a phone call.'

'The telephone is in Monsieur André's study,' was the brief reply as Madame Thiret swept out of the room, taking the children with her.

Claire wandered from room to room until she found a telephone. So this was André's study; she might have known. The walls were covered with photographs of André and the family on holiday here at Arcachon. In many of the pictures he appeared to be surrounded by beautiful girls. Obviously quite a ladies' man, she thought. The sight of his bronzed body in a pair of brief swimming trunks caused her pulse to race. She sat down at the desk and picked up the phone, dialling the number of André's Paris flat. A courteous voice replied.

'This is the residence of Dr Dubois.'

'May I speak to the doctor, please?'

'I'm afraid the doctor is at the hospital. He was called to do an emergency operation.'

'Thank you, I'll ring him there.'

Claire put the phone down, then rang the number of the hospital. After several minutes, she managed to speak to the theatre sister, who told her, in hushed tones, that the doctor could not be disturbed; he was performing an extremely delicate operation.

'Then would you ask him to call me,' said Claire. 'It's most important.'

'Well, in that case, it might be arranged,' conceded the sister grudgingly. 'Give me your name and number.'

Claire went out into the garden, leaving the french windows open so that she could return if she heard the telephone ring. She sat down on a seat under the trees and looked out across the sea. The sun was beginning to set, casting a warm red glow over the water. In the bushes she could hear the clicking of the crickets. It was very peaceful here, but somehow she felt it difficult to relax. For the first time since leaving England, she found herself longing for the bustle of hospital life. She was beginning to feel useless and unwanted. The shrill sound of the telephone brought her back to earth. Quickly she dashed back into the house. It was André, as she had hoped.

'What's the matter?' he said curtly.

'It's Philippe . . .' Claire started to say.

'What's happened?' he interrupted.

'If you'd let me speak, I could explain. Madame Thiret insists that the children sleep in the room next to hers. I can't possibly supervise Philippe's condition when I'm over on the other side of the house.'

André breathed a sigh of relief. 'Is that all? I thought you were going to tell me there was a crisis.'

'But this is a crisis,' insisted Claire. 'How can I nurse Philippe under these conditions?'

'Now calm down,' André said, in a soothing voice. 'There is no need to worry. Madame Thiret knows about Philippe's condition, and she recognises the fact that you are a trained nurse. I trust her implicitly. If there are any danger signs in the night, she will waken you. She has a heart of gold, but it's sometimes difficult to find.'

'I can't imagine it at all,' put in Claire quickly. 'She treats me as if I'm some sort of naughty child.'

André laughed. 'You'll get used to her. I'll try to come down this weekend to get things sorted out. Would that help you?'

'Yes, I think it would,' she replied evenly. 'And the children would enjoy a visit from their uncle.'

'Then at least I shall be assured of a welcome. Tell Madame Thiret I hope to arrive in time for dinner on Friday,' he said. 'Ring me again, if you need me. Goodbye.'

'Goodbye.' Claire put the phone down and sat back in the chair. The dark eyes of André Dubois, in the photograph on the wall, seemed to be staring inside her. She went upstairs to look for Madame Thiret, and found her coming out of the children's room.

'I should like to speak to you, madame,' she said.

'Hush,' whispered the old lady. 'You'll waken

the children. Come into my room.'

She led the way into a large room, overcrowded with photographs, antiques, furniture and bric-a-brac, and motioned to Claire to sit down.

'Now, what is it you want to say?' she asked, not unkindly.

'I've just been speaking to Dr Dubois,' Claire began.

'Indeed, was that necessary?' asked Madame Thiret coldly.

'I think it was,' Claire replied firmly. 'I needed his professional advice. He's coming for the weekend—hopes to be here for dinner on Friday.'

Madame Thiret's face lit up. 'How nice,' she said. 'Is he flying down?'

'I don't know,' said Claire. 'He didn't say.'

'I expect he is. He usually does as he's such a busy man. He has his own private plane, you know,' the old lady added proudly.

'How convenient,' said Claire. 'Does he fly down here often?'

'Not as often as he would like,' said Madame Thiret. 'He was a frequent visitor last summer, of course . . .' her voice trailed away and she stopped, abruptly.

Claire looked at her quizzically. 'Why was that?' she asked.

There was silence for a few seconds, broken only by the ticking of the grandfather clock, and then Madame Thiret continued quietly,

'I don't really know . . . He spent a lot of time

with the children and their English nurse.' There was no disguising her disapproval when she spoke of Claire's predecessor. Abruptly, the old lady stood up and said,

'I think you should go to bed now, young lady. You must be tired after your long journey. Goodnight.' She turned her back on Claire. The interview was obviously over.

Claire walked over to the door and opened it; looking back into the room, she said, 'Goodnight, madame,' but the old lady had disappeared into her bathroom. She went quietly into the children's room next door. They were both sleeping peacefully. Philippe was clutching a battered old teddy bear. Claire wondered if it had belonged to André.

She checked Philippe's pulse and was relieved to find that it was steady, so she went out quietly, and returned to her own room. Suddenly she felt worn out. Stripping off her clothes, she soaked herself in the bath, until her thoughts cleared a little. Something had happened here last summer between André Dubois and the nurse. Whatever it was, it was no concern of hers. She was not going to become involved with him; she would be cool, professional, efficient but distant . . . But that might not be easy. She kept catching a glimpse of an André who was not the arrogant man she had at first imagined. She had to admit he was terribly attractive—but not to her, of course. There were going to be no complications in their relationship.

CHAPTER THREE

NEXT morning Claire was awakened by the children rushing into her room.

'Get up, quickly,' called Simone. 'Madame Thiret says it's time for breakfast.'

She climbed on to Claire's bed and gave her a good morning kiss. Philippe hung back, shyly, by the door. Claire noticed that he was pale and the cyanosis was more marked. She put on her robe and lifted him on to her lap so that she could take his pulse. It was, as she'd thought, irregular. Should she ring André? Perhaps later, if his condition didn't improve.

'Tell Madame Thiret I shall be down as soon as I'm dressed,' she said. 'You can go down to breakfast. I'll join you.'

The children went off down the stairs, leaving Claire to have a quick shower and put on shorts and a tee-shirt. Humming quietly to herself, she went into the dining-room. Madame Thiret looked up in disapproval. Her eyes narrowed ominously as she saw Claire's bare legs and arms.

'Is that the way you dress for breakfast in your country?' she enquired sternly.

Claire gasped. 'On holiday, yes.'

'May I suggest you wear a skirt next time,'

Madame Thiret continued, without looking at Claire.

Claire sat down at the table, wondering how much more she could take from the old lady. If it weren't for Philippe's condition she would pack her bags and go back to England. Fuming inside, she was suddenly aware that Madame Thiret was holding out a large cup of coffee towards her. She took it meekly and said,

'Thank you madame.'

'I thought you might take the children along to the Mickey Club this morning,' said Madame Thiret in a bland voice, as though nothing had happened. 'It's good for them to meet children of their own age.'

'Certainly. I should like that,' said Claire. It would be good to get away from the house for a while. 'What shall I wear?'

Madame Thiret gave a delicate cough. 'I think your present outfit is eminently suitable, for the beach.' She stressed her final words, leaving Claire in no doubt as to the unsuitability of her clothes for the breakfast table.

'Henri will drive you along to the beach,' continued Madame Thiret. 'And he will wait until you are ready to return.'

'Oh, is that necessary?' began Claire, but Madame Thiret's look silenced her.

'Of course it's necessary. The Flament family do not walk along the public highway,' she said sternly. 'It will take you some time to get used to our ways, I think.'

Claire fought back her reply and stood up. 'I'll go and get my things,' she said quietly.

'The children will be ready in five minutes,' said Madame Thiret. 'We shall be in the hall.'

'No,' said Claire firmly. 'I'll come to their room to collect them.'

Madame Thiret looked surprised. 'Very well,' she said.

Claire went to her room and prepared a small bag with medical equipment. She was not going to be caught out in an emergency. When she arrived at the children's room, she found them waiting for her; Madame Thiret was nowhere to be seen. Claire picked Philippe up, and they went down to the car.

Henri drove off along the quiet road until he came to the sea front. It was still early in the season, so the beach was relatively uncrowded. The car stopped at the Mickey Club, with its multicoloured flags and banners, and Henri opened the door for Claire. She stepped out with the children, and they started to make their way across the soft sand.

'I'll wait here for you,' said the chauffeur.

'Thank you, Henri.' Claire led the children over to the area of the beach reserved for the Mickey Club. Several other children were excitedly going inside as she arrived with Simone and Philippe.

'There's no need for you to stay, mademoiselle,' said the young man at the entrance to the club. 'They're quite safe with us.'

'I don't want to leave them,' said Claire. 'The little boy is rather delicate, and may get tired.'

'Well, I don't mind having you around,' said the young man, smiling at her appraisingly. They had been speaking in French, but he suddenly switched languages and said,

'Are you English?'

'Yes,' said Claire. 'Are you?'

'Half and half. My mother's French, my father's English. Patrick Carter.' He held out his hand.

'Claire Baxter.'

'I've spent all my summers here at the Mickey Club; started off playing here when I was a child, and then I got a holiday job, when I was a student.'

'How nice for you,' said Claire. 'Are you still a student?'

'Heavens, no!' he laughed boyishly. 'I graduated three years ago; spent a couple of years working in an office in London, hated it, so I left. I get by with what I earn on my travels. My parents have a house in Arcachon, so I come here in the summer. I wouldn't go back to the old nine-to-five routine for anything. Anyway, I enjoy the work here. Come through and have a look at the equipment.'

They went through to the play area, and Patrick introduced Claire to the other helpers. The morning passed very quickly, with races, competitions and other activities. Patrick played the guitar, and all the children gathered round for a final sing-song before they went home for lunch.

'Are you coming back this afternoon?' Patrick asked Claire.

'No, I don't think so. The children will need a rest.'

'Pity—I'd like to show you round Arcachon afterwards. Are you free tonight?'

Claire thought carefully before answering, 'Not really.'

'But after the children are asleep,' he persisted. 'Can't you leave someone in charge of them?'

'Well, I suppose I could ask Madame Thiret,' she said hesitantly.

'Of course you could—all work and no play isn't good for you.' Patrick smiled broadly, displaying white, even teeth in his deeply sun-tanned face. His smile was infectious, and Claire smiled back at this carefree, happy-go-lucky young man. He seemed to be just what she needed to cheer her up after the sombre, depressing attitude of Madame Thiret.

'OK. I'll pick you up about nine,' he said. 'I know where you live.'

'Do you?' Claire was surprised.

'Everyone knows André Dubois.'

Claire found herself looking forward to the evening. Madame Thiret disapproved, of course, but Claire was determined to be firm with her. She insisted on putting the children to bed herself. When they were asleep, she knocked quietly on Madame Thiret's door. Madame Thiret was sewing, she barely looked up when Claire entered.

'I'll leave the children to you, madame,' said Claire.

The old lady nodded, and continued with her work. 'Don't be late, young lady,' she muttered.

'Of course not,' replied Claire. 'Goodnight.'

Patrick arrived soon afterwards. Claire went out to meet him, and as she did so, she heard Madame Thiret moving along to the children's room. At least she could have peace of mind that her patient was being well cared for while she was away.

A smart-looking, new sports car was standing in the drive. Claire climbed in beside Patrick, wondering how on earth he could afford such luxury on his earnings. The car sped off down the drive, and along the front of the bay, screeching to a halt outside one of the brightly-lit bars. A crowd of young people were gathered round a table in front of the bar. They greeted Patrick noisily. He was obviously very popular with them. He introduced Claire, and called to the waiter to bring more drinks for everyone.

'What will you have, Claire?' he said, and gave a nod of approval when she asked for kir. '*Un kir, deux cafés, un Pernod, trois bières, et un cognac,*' he called out.

The waiter brought the drinks, and the carefree conversation continued round the table, touching on politics, sport, local scandal, and the occasional joke, which Claire sometimes found difficult to understand. However, she enjoyed the relaxed atmosphere; it was good to laugh again.

'I see you've got another new car,' said one of the young men to Patrick.

'Beats me how he can afford it,' said another.

Everyone laughed.

'Yes, I was wondering how . . .' began Claire, innocently.

'What a question!' said one of the girls. 'Patrick doesn't have to manage anything—except his rich father.'

Patrick looked annoyed at this. 'I've never known you to complain about accepting help from me, Cécile,' he said.

'Oh I'm not complaining, darling. There's nothing wrong with having money.' She leaned over and kissed him on the cheek. He seemed somewhat appeased, but glanced at Claire to see what she was thinking.

'My father gives me a generous allowance,' he said defensively.

'You're very lucky,' she said quietly.

'Yes, I suppose I am. Let's have another drink—waiter!'

'No, I really must be going back,' said Claire.

'So soon?'

'I promised to be out for an hour. Madame Thiret is something of a tyrant.'

'I can imagine. I remember seeing her when I was a child and she petrified me,' Patrick laughed. 'Come on, let's go if we have to.' He signalled to the waiter. '*L'addition s'il vous plaît*,' he called, and placed a bank note on the table. 'Goodbye everyone, see you tomorrow.'

There were noisy farewells all round, and then they drove quickly back to the house.

'Will I see you tomorrow?' he said.

'I expect so.' Claire climbed out of the car before he could detain her. 'Thanks for a lovely evening, 'bye.'

She let herself in quietly, and crept up the stairs towards the children's room.

'Is that you, Nurse,' a voice called, as she passed Madame Thiret's room.

Claire sighed, 'Yes it is, madame,'

'There's no need to disturb Philippe—I've just been in to see him.'

'Thank you, madame,' said Claire patiently. 'I won't disturb him, but I'd like to look for myself.'

There was no reply to this; Claire did not expect one. She went into Philippe's room and made a careful check on his condition. When she was quite satisfied, she went across to her own room.

What a pleasant evening I've had, she thought. It's so nice to meet an uncomplicated man, who enjoys life so much.

The next day, she spent another morning at the Mickey Club with the children. Her new friends now accepted her as one of the team. Philippe started to move about amongst the other children, and under Claire's watchful eye he began to try new experiences, and make new friends. Simone joined in everything, of course—nothing wrong with her health, thought Claire.

When they got back, they found Madame Thiret in the kitchen, supervising the lunch. She was tearing a strip off the maid and the cook about the state of the kitchen. They retreated into the dining-room.

Lunch was served by a very subdued maid. The children ate quietly, sensing the tension in the atmosphere.

'What time will Uncle André be here?' asked Simone tentatively, after several minutes' silence.

'Not until after you're in bed,' said Madame Thiret severely.

Simone pulled a face. 'Can't we stay up until he comes?'

'Certainly not,' said the old housekeeper. 'It will be much too late for you. Nurse Baxter, will you be staying in tonight?'

'Of course,' said Claire.

'We shall dine at nine o'clock, if the doctor is here by then.'

'Very good, madame,' Claire experienced a wave of panic. Dinner with Madame Thiret and the formidable André Dubois was not going to be easy.

She felt uneasy and apprehensive throughout the rest of the day. The children did not want to go to bed without seeing their uncle, and Claire had to coax them by promising she would ask him to take them out tomorrow. After they were settled, she went to her room and bathed, and changed into a white, broderie anglais dress, cool, casual and very becoming. She couldn't understand why it was taking her so long to prepare for the evening.

It's probably nerves at the thought of the impending ordeal, Claire told herself. She was so absorbed that she didn't hear the car pull into the drive. As she struggled to fasten the clasp on her necklace, there was a knock on her door.

'*Entrez*,' she called automatically, and then gasped as she saw the reflection of André Dubois in her mirror. The necklace slipped from her fingers on to the dressing-table. Her discomfort seemed to amuse him; with long, easy strides he crossed the room.

'I hope I'm not disturbing you—here let me do that.' The delicate, sensitive fingers of the surgeon picked up the necklace and clasped it firmly around her neck. Claire stared fixedly into the dressing-table mirror, and saw that André was watching her reflection too.

'It's a beautiful necklace,' he said, as he secured the clasp on the filigree silver. The touch of his fingers on her neck sent shivers down her spine. She sat absolutely still until the strange feeling had passed.

'It belonged to my grandmother,' she said quickly. 'Did you want to see me about something?'

'Yes, I wanted to ask you about Philippe; how is he?' he said.

'His condition is stable at the moment, but I don't like the irregular pulse and the cyanosis,' said Claire, cool and efficient on the outside.

'Nor do I; I think I'll take him into hospital for tests when we get back to Paris. Let him enjoy his holiday here, but continue to watch him carefully.'

His gaze swept around the room. 'And how about you?'

'Me? I'm all right,' she answered in a surprised voice.

'No problems with Madame Thiret?' he asked.

'What sort of problems?' said a voice from the doorway. They both turned to find the old housekeeper standing erect and forbidding on the threshold.

'Ah, there you are,' said André, as he walked towards her, kissing her lightly on both cheeks.

'I didn't expect to find you in this young lady's bedroom,' she said sternly. 'And what sort of problems are you talking about?'

'Simply discussing our patient,' said André smoothly. 'Let's all go downstairs and have a drink.' He took the old lady by the arm, and helped her down the stairs. Claire followed them as soon as she had regained her composure.

They drank their aperitifs in the drawing-room, and then went into dinner. The meal seemed endless. Claire felt excluded, as Madame Thiret and André talked on and on about the time when he was a boy. They lingered over coffee at the table, and Madame Thiret fetched cigars and brandy. She poured a glass for André, but did not offer one to Claire.

Suddenly remembering her promise to the children, Claire said, 'Do you think you could take the children out tomorrow? They were so disappointed at not seeing you.'

'Yes, I think I can spare them a few hours. After all, that's why I'm here. Will you come with us?'

Claire was startled. 'If you'd like me to,' she said.

'Of course. I can't cope with them by myself, especially if we go sailing.'

'Sailing? Oh André, do you think that's wise?' said Madame Thiret anxiously. 'I don't think you should take Philippe.'

'Nonsense! He'll be perfectly all right with Nurse Baxter and me. Do him good, won't it, Nurse?'

'If you say so,' she said, avoiding those deep, searching eyes.

'That's settled then,' said André. He seemed to be watching her carefully.

Madame Thiret rose from the table. 'It's time I went to my bed,' she said, then turning to Claire she added, 'I think you should got to bed now. Monsieur André has had a hard day—he wishes to relax.'

'No, no, don't go,' André put a restraining hand on Claire's arm as he looked firmly at Madame Thiret. 'I should prefer to have someone to talk to,' he said evenly.

Madame Thiret's mouth set in a firm line.

'As you wish, but please don't stay up too late, my boy,' she said quietly.

When the old lady had gone, André smiled at Claire.

'Would you like a brandy?'

'No thank you,' she said. 'I think I should be going to bed.'

'It's much too early. Besides, we didn't finish our conversation. I shall pour a brandy for you—doctor's orders,' he added, as she started to protest. 'It'll help you to relax. You look very tense tonight. Is Madame Thiret giving you a hard time?'

'Oh, I can handle her,' said Claire, and without thinking, she raised the glass to her lips. As she sipped the smooth, golden liquid, she started to unwind.

'She seems to dislike me,' she continued.

'That's only her manner; she's very abrupt.' André had moved closer to her. Suddenly he reached across and took hold of her hand. The quick movement startled her, and she put down the brandy glass, spilling some of the contents as she did so.

'No need to worry,' he smiled. 'I was only going to say that it's not been easy for you to settle in here, but you seem to be making a good job of it.'

'As good as my predecessor?' she asked quietly.

He froze, removed his hand, and stood up.

'I see Madame Thiret has been talking to you, so there's nothing I can add to the subject.' He turned and walked quickly over to the french window. 'I'm going for a walk. I'll see you in the morning. Have the children ready by nine o'clock. Goodnight.'

Claire watched the tall, handsome figure walk away towards the sea glistening in the moonlight.

She had an almost uncontrollable desire to run after him. She remembered the feel of his fingers on her hand just now, and on her neck, as he fastened her necklace.

Steady on, she told herself, he was only trying to make up for being so unpleasant when I first arrived. I wonder how he behaved towards the nurse last year . . . I wonder . . . Oh, heavens! The tall figure in the moonlight had turned round and was coming back. He came in through the windows.

'I'm glad you're still there. I think perhaps I owe you an explanation, about Nurse Johnson.' He came over to her chair and put his hand lightly on the back of it.

'Nurse Johnson?'

'Yes, Pat Johnson, the girl who was here last year. She was extremely difficult—a very complicated person.'

'So it would seem—I'm really not interested,' said Claire.

'The thing is,' he continued quietly, 'you mustn't believe everything you hear.'

'I won't,' said Claire, and stood up quickly. The nearness of his body behind her chair was too much. She walked over to the door.

'Goodnight.' Her heart was pounding as she climbed the stairs. She went into her room and closed the door. What was it André had said to her? You mustn't believe everything you hear. She would remember that.

CHAPTER FOUR

CLAIRE awoke the next morning with a pleasant feeling of anticipation. Ah yes, today we're going sailing, she remembered. She jumped out of bed and went over to the window. As she drew back the curtains the morning sun, already warm, streamed in across the window sill. Opening the windows wide, she breathed in the refreshing air, discerning that slight, unmistakable salty tang of the sea. She could see the waves were tumbling gently on to the sea-shore and there wasn't a cloud in the sky.

Mm, it's good to be alive on a day like this, she thought. Now what shall I wear? No point in offending Madame Thiret again. Something sober and suitable for breakfast, then I can change into sailing clothes afterwards.

She put on a cool white cotton dress which buttoned up to the neck, and white sandals. Looking in the mirror, she smiled. I almost look as if I'm back in hospital! she thought.

She skipped lightly down the stairs and across to the children's room. The house was very quiet, but from the kitchen came the sound of the maids' voices, and the delicious aroma of freshly ground coffee. Claire opened the door of the children's room and went in. Simone was still sleeping peacefully, but Philippe was wide awake, his wistful eyes gazing up at the ceiling. He smiled happily when he saw Claire and sat up in bed.

'*Bonjour* mademoiselle,' he said politely and reached out one of his thin pale hands towards her, as any well-brought-up young French boy should.

Claire shook his hand solemnly. This boy is old beyond his years, she thought sadly. There isn't enough fun in his life. She sat on the edge of the bed and took his pulse. She found to her relief that it was fairly regular, his skin was a good colour, and there was no evidence of cyanosis. Smiling down at the tiny boy who was looking anxiously up at her she said, 'Uncle André is going to take us sailing today.'

His fact lit up with pleasure. 'Is he going to take me?' he asked incredulously.

'Yes, of course,' said Claire, pleased with his reaction.

'He usually leaves me behind, because I'm a nuisance. Are you sure he's taking me?'

Claire's heart went out in sympathy to him. 'Of course he's taking you, and you're not a nuisance,' was her reassuring reply.

'Nurse Johnson thought I was. She always used to leave me with Madame Thiret,' he said quietly.

'Well, er . . . you were younger then,' she said quickly. 'This year you can do more exciting things. Would you like to waken Simone for me?'

'Oh, yes.' The small boy climbed out of bed and walked importantly across to his sister. Shaking her gently he said, 'Simone, would you like to come sailing with us today?'

The little girl stirred in her sleep and opened her big blue eyes. 'Sailing?' she asked. 'Are we going sailing?'

'Yes, mademoiselle says we can go sailing with Uncle André.'

Simone shot out of bed and rushed across to Claire, flinging her little arms round her.

'Oh thank you, mademoiselle, I love sailing.'

'Well let's get a move on then,' said Claire. 'I want both of you in the bathroom now, come on.'

As soon as the children were ready Claire took them down to breakfast. André and Madame Thiret were already sitting at the table. The children greeted their uncle noisily and both tried to climb on to his lap at the same time.

'*Ça suffit*, that's enough,' said Madame Thiret sternly. She turned to Claire. 'You mustn't allow the children to be so excited' she said. 'I heard you getting them ready this morning, they were making far too much noise.'

'Oh, they're just happy to see me, that's all,' said André calmly, as he settled his nephew and niece at the table, one on either side of him. 'And I'm happy to see them too. Did mademoiselle tell you we're going sailing today?'

'*Mais oui, bien sûr*,' said the children simultaneously, their eyes shining with excitement.

'But first you must eat your *petit déjeuner*,' said Madame Thiret, placing bowls of hot chocolate and pieces of crusty French bread in front of the children. '*Bon appétit, mes enfants.*'

Breakfast continued in a more peaceful atmosphere. Claire drank her coffee and ate a delicious fresh roll with butter and apricot jam. She was conscious that André was looking at her but was determined not to speak until she was spoken to. After several minutes' silence he said, 'You're looking very professional this morning, Nurse. I do hope you're going to change your dress before you come sailing.'

Claire took a deep breath and avoided Madame Thiret's eyes as she said, 'Of course I'm going to change, but I couldn't possibly wear sailing clothes at the breakfast table.' She looked at André and saw that his eyes were twinkling mischievously.

'No, no, of course not,' he said understandingly.

Madame Thiret nodded in approval, quite unaware that she was the object of their amusement.

After breakfast Claire got the children ready, then changed into shorts and a tee-shirt. She packed a small box of toys for the children, and a small emergency bag, before taking everything down into the hall. Madame Thiret had produced a huge picnic box which Henri was loading into the car.

Soon they were driving along the sea front towards the marina. Pleasure boats of all kinds were moored in neat rows alongside the wooden walkways which stretched out like the teeth of a comb from the granite harbour wall. There were luxury yachts, powerful motor-cruisers, sleek racing yachts, small dinghies and family holiday boats.

On the far side of the harbour, near to the town, Claire could see the commercial fishing boats. The jetty was very wide, with small sheds on the harbourside for storage. Underneath the wall on the seaward side of the jetty was a long row of cars and they found a space near to the gangway where André's boat was moored.

Henri unloaded the car and helped André to carry everything along to the boat. Claire had her hands full trying to manoeuvre the children along the narrow wooden walkway to the boat.

When Claire saw the yacht she was rather surprised. She had expected something far more luxurious. On either side were two huge modern motor-cruisers, each of which could have slept ten, gleaming with white paint and topped by a variety of radar aerials and electronic equipment. André's yacht, by contrast, was obviously much older and was made entirely of wood, which although varnished, looked somehow old-fashioned.

'It's a pre-war twelve metre,' said André with obvious pride as he clambered aboard.

The main cabin was adequate, but small and functional, with two bunks which served as couches during the day, a dining table and a small map table by the hatch. Through the door there was a galley, a bathroom and two small cabins, each with a double bunk.

'Do you like it?' André asked Claire.

'Yes, it's full of character,' she said.

'Exactly.' He seemed pleased at her assessment. 'That's why I've kept it all these years. It used to be my father's. I wouldn't change it for anything. Beautiful old thing it is,' he said lovingly. 'Come on, would you like to put life-jackets on the children please? Then we can be off.'

He clambered about organising the boat, as happy as a young schoolboy on his day off. Starting the engine, he negotiated his craft expertly out of the marina into the bay. When they were clear of the other boats he shut off the engines.

There was a good breeze and the sails billowed healthily as André set the course straight down the centre of the Bay of Arcachon and out into the sea. They sailed round the corner, past Pyla sur Mer and along towards Pilat Plage, with its golden sands shining in the sunlight.

'Look at the huge dune,' called André, pointing out the enormous hill of sand which rose up behind the beach. 'It's the biggest sand dune in the world.'

The children were jumping up and down in excitement and Claire was glad they were wearing life-jackets.

'A little further along we shall come to a marvellous beach,' André was saying. 'It's usually quite deserted, because it's difficult to get to by land. We'll have our picnic there, would you like that children?'

'Oh yes, and can we play in the sand?' shouted Simone.

'Of course you can,' he said happily.

They sailed along the coast until André called excitedly, 'There it is, there's the beach I told you about.'

He headed the boat towards the shore until they reached the shallow water, where he stopped and weighed anchor. Then, putting the picnic box into the dinghy, he helped Claire and the children to climb in.

As soon as they reached the shore, the children jumped happily into the warm, soft sand. 'Can we take these off now?' said Philippe to Claire, as he struggled with his life-jacket.

'Of course you can,' said Claire, deftly removing the cumbersomejackets from the two children.

André pulled the dinghy well up on the shore and started to unload the things. Claire produced buckets and spades from one of the boxes, and soon the children were happily engrossed in making sand-castles.

'How about a swim, before lunch?' said André to Claire.

'Lovely, but what about the children?'

'They'll be all right. We can keep an eye on them if we don't go out too far.'

Claire slipped off her shorts and tee-shirt, thankful that she was already wearing her bikini.

There was no mistaking the appraising look André gave her as she ran down the beach into the sea. His eyes shone with admiration as he followed the slim, lithe figure in the white bikini.

The water felt chilly after the warmth of the

beach, but as soon as Claire had swum a few strokes she started to feel warm again. André quickly caught up with her and they swam side by side.

'Mustn't go too far out,' said Claire. 'We mightn't hear the children.' She turned and trod water for a few seconds, so that she could watch the small figures on the beach. They were still playing happily together. She lay on her back and gazed up at the blue sky.

'Do you like it here?' asked André.

'Mm, it's so peaceful,' she murmured.

There was no sound except the lapping of the gentle waves on the shore and the occasional playful cry from the children. André turned over to lie on his back next to her. As he did so their hands touched in the water. Claire shivered, but it had nothing to do with the temperature of the water.

'Are you cold?' asked André.

'A little,' she lied, moving quickly away from him. 'Let's go back to the children.' She struck out at a swift pace but André reached the shore before her. He waited until she came out of the waves, and they ran up the beach to the children. Simone took hold of Claire's hand.

'*Regarde le château,*' she said, proudly pointing to the pile of sand they had made.

'*C'est magnifique,*' said Claire enthusiastically, as she knelt down in the sand. 'Let's put some towers on it.' She filled one of the buckets with sand and carefully placed it on top of the castle. When she removed the bucket, Philippe clapped his hands in delight.

'*Encore*,' he cried.

Simone had already picked up a bucket and was making her own towers, but Philippe was quite happy to watch Claire make them for him.

André smiled down at the happy little group. 'I think I'll go and see what delights Madame Thiret has put in the picnic box,' he said.

'Oh, would you like me to help you?' Claire started to get up from the sand.

'No, no, you stay and amuse the children. You seem very good at it. A natural, I would say.'

There was a look of tenderness in the dark eyes which met Claire's and she turned hastily away to resume her task with renewed vigour.

The popping of a champagne cork made Claire jump. She looked up and saw André laughing at her, several yards away, where he was preparing the picnic.

'Come and have a drink before lunch,' he called, as he poured the champagne into two glasses.

Dusting the sand from her hands, Claire went across to join him and took the glass he handed to her.

'*Santé,*' he said, as he raised his glass.

'Mm, it's deliciously cold,' she said in surprise.

'Of course it's cold,' he said, indicating the ice-bucket. 'I always bring ice with me. No one should ever have to drink warm champagne, even on a desert island.'

Claire laughed. 'It is rather like a desert island.' she said, casting a glance round the vast areas of deserted sand. She sat down on the large rush mat which André had spread out ready for the picnic. He sat down beside her and they sipped their champagne in silence for a few minutes, enjoying the peaceful beauty of the bay. The sun shone warmly down and Claire felt her skin tingling with the dried salt of the sea water.

'More champagne?' said André, reaching for the bottle.

'Careful,' she laughed. 'I'm not used to champagne. My head feels quite light already.'

'Champagne is very good for you,' said André as he refilled the glasses, and replaced the bottle in the ice-bucket.

Simone came running over to them. 'I'm thirsty.'

'Well I can't give you any champagne, *chérie*,' said André, smiling at his little niece.

'There's some fruit juice in this box,' said Claire. She found glasses and poured drinks for the children. 'Philippe, come and have a drink,' she called.

The little boy padded gently over the sand and sank down wearily beside Claire. She put her arm round him and gave him some juice, which he drank slowly.

'Are you tired?' she asked anxiously.

'Mm.' He snuggled closer to Claire and closed his eyes.

'You can have a sleep after lunch,' said André. 'Look what Madame Thiret has prepared for us.'

Philippe opened his eyes, but showed very little enthusiasm for the food which André was spreading out in front of them, whereas Simone was already holding out her plate.

'*Du poulet pour moi*,' she shouted happily as André started to carve the chicken. He placed a piece of the succulent white meat on Simone's plate and she started to eat hungrily.

Claire prepared a small portion of the tender chicken for Philippe and coaxed him into eating it, but the effort of this at the end of his strenuous morning left him exhausted. He lay down beside Claire, so she covered him gently with a towel and let him sleep.

'Madame Thiret has excelled herself this time,' said André as he served a crisp green salad to follow the chicken. Claire found some vinaigrette dressing, already prepared in a jar, for the salad, and some potato crisps. The crusty French bread had survived the journey very well, and was still surprisingly fresh. There was an apple tart and a carton of cream for dessert and some excellent cheese, stored in a cold container.

'You must try some of this Camembert,' said André, 'It's exactly ripe.'

'Ripe?' asked Claire, thinking that it was a funny word to describe cheese.

'Oh, yes, Camembert has to be ripe before you can eat it. Of course, we should have a nice Bordeaux to go with it,' he said.

'Oh, I know nothing about wine,' she said honestly. 'I just know this tastes good.'

'I can teach you,' he said quietly. 'If you stay around long enough. It's not a subject that can be learned about quickly—one needs time.'

For several seconds their eyes met, then Claire looked away, gazing out at the foam-topped waves as they tumbled on to the shore. She had detected a certain earnestness in his voice which she could not, or would not understand. She lay on her back looking up at the sky and saw that there was still not a cloud to be seen. It was a perfect day in every way. Suddenly she was aware that Simone was pulling on her hand.

'Come and play in the sand with me,' the little girl was saying.

'Sh, don't disturb Philippe,' said Claire gently. 'He needs to rest.'

'I think Simone should have a rest too,' said André briskly. 'We'll take the children back to the boat. They'll be more comfortable in the cabin.'

'Oh, all right, if you think it's necessary,' Claire was loath to leave the idyllic beach. The mellowing effect of the champagne had made her feel drowsy, and she would have liked to stay stretched out on the sand forever. André started to pack away the picnic into the boxes, so Claire forced herself to stand up and help him.

When the boxes were all loaded into the dinghy she lifted Philippe into her arms and carried him across the sand. Simone skipped along by André's side.

Soon they were skimming through the water, back to the yacht. Claire took her precious bundle down into the main cabin and laid him on one of the bunks, covering him with a light sheet. Then she asked Simone to creep in quietly and lie down on the bunk at the other side of the cabin. The little girl was beginning to feel sleepy and was quite happy to settle down under the cool sheet. She smiled as Claire tucked her in and reached up to give her a kiss, before closing her eyes.

Claire went up on deck, and saw that André had unpacked the dinghy. He was holding the champagne bottle and two glasses.

'It's a pity to waste the last of the champagne,' he said. 'The bubbles won't keep, you know. Here you are.' He handed her a glass of the sparkling liquid.

Claire laughed as she took the glass. 'You talked me into it,' she giggled. 'You're a very persuasive man.'

As she sank down on the cushions at the front of the boat she said, 'I hope you don't want me to do any work for a while. I don't think I could concentrate on anything at the moment.'

'No, we don't need to set off for another hour or so. We can stay anchored here and relax,' he said as he stretched out on the seat opposite Claire. 'Mm, this is the life.'

Neither of them spoke for a few minutes. The boat rocked gently on the calm water. There was a slight sea breeze which helped to cool the rays of the hot sun.

Claire was the first to break the silence. 'I thought it was perfect on the beach, but it's even better out here on the sea,' she murmured sleepily.

André raised himself on to his elbow and looked across at her. 'I've enjoyed bringing you out here, Claire. It's good to be with someone who's so full of *joie de vivre*.'

Claire smiled back at him. 'At the moment I feel very sleepy,' she said, closing her eyes. 'Waken me when it's time to cast off, or whatever it is we have to do.'

André gently removed the champagne glass before it could slip from her fingers.

Some time later she opened her eyes to see André standing over her.

'I think it's time we were on our way, if we're to catch the tide,' he said.

She stirred and stretched luxuriously on the seat.

'You look like a kitten awaking from a deep sleep,' he said, placing his hand lightly on her hair and running his fingers gently through it. 'Mm, it's smooth as silk, just like a kitten's.'

Claire smiled and sat up, swinging her legs off the seat as she started to stand up, but being a little unsteady she fell against André.

He caught hold of her and held her to him. 'Take your time Claire, no need to hurry,' he said. 'The champagne and the sun have made you dizzy.'

His arms were still holding her and she caught her breath as he leaned her gently back on the cushions. Suddenly he bent forward and kissed her cheek lightly. In that moment she felt herself hopelessly lost. She found herself responding to the nearness of his hard body. Her head told her to disentangle herself, but her heart wanted to stay in his warm embrace.

His mouth moved gently over to hers and she responded naturally to the gentle pressure of his parted lips. Everything seemed so unreal as she abandoned herself to the ecstasy of his kiss.

It was only the sound of the children moving around in the cabin, that brought her back to reality.

She stirred helplessly in his arms. 'André, the children are awake,' she said, trying to sit up.

He released her, running his fingers through her hair again. 'Too bad,' he said, with a wry grin. 'I should have wakened you earlier. OK Florence Nightingale, go and look after the babes and then we'll set sail.'

Claire went into the cabin, put the children back into their life-jackets and brought them up on deck. There was a feeling of unutterable peace as the sails billowed in the wind. She sat in the front of the boat with the children, hardly daring to look at André.

They sailed back round the coast and into the smooth water of the Bay of Arcachon. The marina seemed a hive of activity after the peaceful sea voyage. André tied up the boat and Claire climbed out with the children. 'Leave the things,' he said. 'I'll get Henri to help me unload.'

They had just started along the walkway when a

woman's voice called out, 'André!'

A tall slim, dark-haired young woman was standing on the deck of a luxurious yacht in the next gangway.

André stood quite still. 'Pat Johnson,' he said in surprise. 'What on earth are you doing here?'

'I'm on holiday,' said the elegant woman. 'Staying with friends.'

The children seemed to be clinging a little more tightly to Claire's hands.

André bent down towards his nephew. 'You remember Nurse Johnson, don't you,' he said.

'Yes,' said Philippe, then quietly he whispered to Claire. 'Can we go home now?'

The brittle voice across the water was continuing.

'Aren't you going to introduce me to your friend?'

'Why of course . . . Pat Johnson meet Claire Baxter.'

André seemed strangely ill at ease, but Pat Johnson was obviously enjoying the situation.

'Why don't you both come back to my hotel for a drink? Bring the children, if you like.'

'Oh we couldn't possibly do that.' Claire spoke quickly, feeling suddenly tired and bedraggled after her day in the open air. She wondered how Pat Johnson managed to look so band-box fresh. 'I mean, I couldn't bring the children—they're very tired,' she added.

'I'll come for a drink with you,' said André quietly. 'Take the children back to the car, Nurse

Baxter, and ask Henri to fetch the things from the boat.' The change in his manner was like a slap in the face.

Claire gasped audibly. 'Why certainly, sir,' she said with a calmness which she did not feel. 'Come along children.'

Pat Johnson was smiling happily and already tripping elegantly along the walkway. 'I'll meet you on the quayside André,' she called.

Claire held the children tightly by the hand as she negotiated the narrow wooden planks back to the car. She felt the strong hot tears pricking behind her eyes and knew that she must not look back at André. He was only her employer after all. If he wanted to go for a drink, why shouldn't he? She mustn't get carried away by a romantic interlude over a bottle of champagne.

The faithful Henri was waiting for her on the quayside. He came forward with a concerned look on his face when he saw Claire and the children.

'Why, mademoiselle, you're all alone. Where is Monsieur *le docteur*?'

'He's just met a friend of his. They're going for a drink,' she said quickly. 'Would you fetch the things from the boat Henri?'

'Why of course, mademoiselle, but first I'm going to take you home. You look very tired. I'll return and see to the boat later—it will take some time to unload and moor it properly.'

He opened the door of the car and Claire climbed thankfully into the back seat, settling the children one on either side of her. Henri started the engine and the car purred its way along the marina and back to the house.

When they arrived, Madame Thiret also expressed her concern that they were alone.

'Monsieur *le docteur*, *où est-il*?' she enquired anxiously.

'Monsieur *le docteur* met a friend,' said Claire wearily. 'Pat Johnson.'

Madame Thiret's mouth set in a thin line. 'I see. Well, I suppose it was to be expected.' She turned to Claire. 'Perhaps you would like to prepare the children for supper mademoiselle. I thought we could all dine early this evening, after your long day in the open air.'

'That was very thoughtful of you, madame. I should like that,' said Claire truthfully.

She went to her room and hastily slipped a skirt over her shorts, then, after washing the children's hands, she took them into supper.

'I'm afraid we're all rather untidy,' said Claire.

Madame Thiret gave her a kindly smile. 'Don't worry my dear. You must have had a tiring day. Early to bed tonight, I think, for all of you.'

The maid brought in a huge bowl of steaming vegetable soup which she placed in front of Madame Thiret. The old lady picked up a large spoon and served generous helpings in the blue and white porcelain bowls.

Claire found the soup warm and soothing. She began to unwind and felt almost relaxed again, when Madame Thiret's voice broke in on her thoughts.

'Tell me about Nurse Johnson.'

Claire put down her soup spoon and looked across the table at the old lady.

'What do you want to know?' she asked quietly.

'Well, what did she look like today and where have they gone together?' The words came out in a rush.

'She looked . . . er, she looked . . . elegant,' Claire said lamely. 'And they've gone for a drink at her hotel, I think.' She bent her head over her soup bowl.

'Hm.' Madame Thiret sniffed. 'I might have known she'd come back,' then suddenly remembering that the children were there, she turned to them and said, 'Eat up your soup, *mes enfants*. It's time you were in bed.'

There was no main course that evening, for which Claire was truly grateful. The maid served small dishes of crème caramel, after which Claire said she would like to put the children to bed.

'Will you take coffee before you go up?' asked Madame Thiret.

'No thank you, madame. I'm very tired. Goodnight.'

Taking the children by the hand she went up to their room. It wasn't long before they were safely tucked into bed, and on the point of sleep. Claire tiptoed quietly out and went to her own room, thankfully closing the door.

She took a shower and then lay on her bed trying to read a book, but as she turned the pages, none of the words seemed to stick in her mind.

Some time later the sound of tyres screeching on the drive told her that André had returned. She heard raised voices downstairs, one of them being that of Madame Thiret who sounded extremely angry.

No need to get involved, she thought, but it's a pity it had to end like this.

The moon was shining in through the gap in the curtains, casting a pale glow around the room.

The end of a perfect day, she thought. . . . and the end of something that never even began.

She closed her eyes and tried to sleep.

CHAPTER FIVE

NEXT morning the sun was shining again in a clear blue sky but Claire found that her *joie de vivre* of the day before had vanished.

Work, that's what I need, she thought. Something to keep me totally occupied. Quickly she dressed and went along to the children's room. Soon, in the midst of their childish cries of joy and delight in the new day, she lost the feeling of unease and her natural good humour returned. If ever I get married, I shall have six children she decided, as she skipped happily down the stairs, a child on either side of her.

André was just leaving the dining-room and the children bumped into him in the doorway. 'Steady on,' he snapped in a bad-tempered voice. 'Really Nurse, I do wish you would exert more control over the children.'

Claire stared at him in disbelief. Was this really the same man she had spent the day with yesterday?

His eyes were cold and hard, showing no emotion. 'I take it the children are in good health this morning. Any problems?' he asked in his super-efficient, professional voice.

The children had become very quiet and at first Claire could not bring herself to speak then, remembering that he was after all her employer and also a famous surgeon, used to being treated with respect, she said quietly, 'Nothing I can't handle.'

With that, she took the children to their places at the table and started to pour out their hot chocolate, with an air of complete detachment which she certainly did not feel. When she dared to raise her eyes, she saw that the tall figure in the doorway had gone.

Madame Thiret, who had been to Mass, arrived when they were half-way through breakfast. She smiled approvingly at Claire.

'*Bonjour* mademoiselle,' she said.

'*Bonjour* madame. *Du café*?' Claire picked up the silver coffee-pot.

'*Oui, s'il vous plaît.*' The old lady settled herself in her chair. She looked somehow older and more frail this morning, as she accepted the coffee cup from Claire.

After several minutes' silence Madame Thiret said, 'He's going sailing again,' adding ominously, 'with *her*.'

'Her?' asked Claire innocently, but she knew what the reply would be, even before the old lady blurted it out.

'Pat Johnson of course.'

'I see.' Claire busied herself putting butter on a roll for Philippe.'

The children had started to listen in, so Claire thought it best to change the subject.

'What would you like to do today children?'

'Let's go to the beach,' they both clamoured.

'There's no need to go all the way to Arcachon,' said Madame Thiret. 'It's always crowded on Sundays. The children will be perfectly happy here on our own private beach.'

Claire felt relieved that today was going to be a fairly simple day. After breakfast it was very easy to walk down through the garden with the children. They took their buckets and spades and amused themselves until lunchtime, needing only occasional help from Claire.

It was a delightful little beach, bounded on one side by tall pine trees and rocks, and having a sweeping view across the bay of Arcachon. There was a great deal of activity on the sea but Claire forced herself not to think about the tall figure out there on the water. Yesterday already seemed like a dream, something which hadn't really happened.

When she took the children back to the house at lunchtime Claire found Madame Thiret greeted her almost affectionately. The cold reserve had gone and it was as if there was a real bond of friendship between them.

After lunch, while the children were sleeping, Claire took a book and went into the garden to read under the trees. The heat of the day had made her feel sleepy and the ringing of the telephone seemed far away in the distance. She was suddenly aware that the maid was standing in front of her.

'*C'est pour vous,* mademoiselle.'

Claire shook herself awake and hurried through

the french windows to the telephone. She recognised the voice at the other end at once.

'Robert, why hello. How did you get my number?' she said.

'I rang Dr Dubois' apartment and his maid gave it to me,' was the reply.

'How's life in gay Paree?' she asked.

'Not very exciting without you,' he said. 'When are you coming back?'

'We've only been here a few days. I'll be back in another week or so.'

'What have you been doing with yourself?' Robert asked.

'Looking after the children, sailing . . .'

'Sailing? I didn't think you knew anything about sailing.'

'I don't,' she laughed. 'Dr Dubois took me out in his boat, and he did all the work—I just sat there.'

'I see. All part of the job eh?' his voice sounded sarcastic.

'Yes, you could say that,' she said lightly.

There was a pause.

'Did you want anything in particular?' asked Claire.

'No, I just wanted to talk to you. We must get together when you come back. I'll show you around Paris.'

'I'd like that,' said Claire.

'Goodbye then. See you soon.'

As she replaced the receiver she found herself longing to get back to Paris, away from all this—all what? She felt she was caught up in the middle of something she didn't understand.

André returned from sailing in the early evening, alone. Claire was playing with the children in the garden as she saw the tall sunburnt figure get out of the car. He strolled slowly across the path towards them. The children took no notice of him, they had not yet forgotten the sharp reprimand of the morning.

He smiled at Claire. 'Have you had a good day?' he asked.

'Yes, thank you,' said Claire, in a polite but distant voice.

'And the children, both well I hope?'

'Yes, no problems,' said Claire.

'Hey you two, don't I get a kiss?'

The children looked uncertainly at their uncle, then cautiously reached up. He picked them up, one in each arm, and hugged them.

'See, we're friends again.' He smiled at Claire.

'Children have very short memories,' she said quietly. 'It's time for me to take them inside.'

'Let me help you. I'd like to examine Philippe before I go.' He carried them inside and up to their room.

Claire undressed Philippe and put the tiny figure on his bed, so that André could make a full examination. After several minutes he declared that he was quite satisfied.

'You seem to be having a good effect on the patient,' he said to Claire quietly, as he removed his stethoscope. 'I still think we'd better do some tests when you get back to Paris.' He turned in the doorway. 'I'm going out for dinner tonight and I shall be leaving early tomorrow morning so I'll say goodbye.'

'Goodbye,' said Claire. She turned to take the children into the bathroom.

'Ring me if you're worried about anything,' he added.

'Of course.' Claire was completely in charge of the situation. Cool, professional, unflappable; she wondered how she could possibly have allowed herself to get carried away with romantic ideas.

The next day she took the children to the Mickey Club. It was good to meet Patrick and her new friends again, she enjoyed the children's laughter and the happy atmosphere of the club. There was no time to think, as she threw herself into all the activities.

After lunch, Madame Thiret asked Claire if she would like the afternoon off. 'I'll look after the children, they can have their rest and then I'll amuse them until you return,' she said kindly.

'That would be nice. Yes, thank you madame.' It would be good to get away, she thought.

Putting on her white slacks and a coral pink shirt she was soon walking along the road into Arcachon. She had no idea what she was going to do. Simply to have some time to herself was sheer bliss. She was beginning to realise the drawbacks of private nursing, where there are no set off-duty times. The work seemed easier than hospital work but the responsibilities were so ill-defined.

Claire reached the town to find that many of the shops were closed in the heat of the afternoon. She found one department store that was open, however, and wandered around looking at clothes and shoes. When she came to the beachwear department she found the most fabulous bikini. It was displayed on one of the models in the middle of the room and Claire stood in front of it trying to make up her mind. She had come out with no intention of buying anything, but this was so beautiful. It was in a cream lycra material which looked like silk, with a delicate gold leaf motif, on which gold beading had been hand-stitched. It was quite impraticable of course but Claire started to visualise herself wearing it. She asked how much it was and reeled at the astronomical price. Still, it's so beautiful, she thought . . .

'I'll take it,' she heard herself saying and watched in amazement as the delicate bikini was wrapped in tissue paper.

'*C'est un cadeau* madame? Is it a gift?' asked the young shop assistant.

'*Mais oui, bien sûr*,' said Claire gaily. Well it was a gift to herself.

'In that case, I'll gift-wrap it for you,' said the girl, carefully placing the bundle of tissue paper inside a pretty box which she wrapped in coloured paper, finishing off with a bow of ribbon.

Claire felt completely light-hearted as she stepped outside the shop. She swung the pretty box by its ribbon and stepped smartly along the pavement. After walking a few yards she came to a small café, with tables outside, and decided to celebrate her new purchase. She sat down at one of the tables under the awning and started to unwrap the paper. It seemed a pity to undo all the shop assistant's careful packing but she just had to have another look at the bikini.

She was so engrossed in her task that she didn't notice a tall elegant figure stop in front of the café.

'So we meet again.'

Claire looked up on hearing the brittle voice, to see Pat Johnson standing by her table.

'Do you mind if I join you?' she said.

'No . . . not at all.' Claire started to push the bikini back in its box.

'What have we here? My, my, that's pretty.' Pat Johnson reached a beautifully manicured hand across and picked up the top part of the bikini. 'Planning a seduction, are you?'

Claire gasped, then recovering her composure, she firmly replaced the bikini in its box.

'I was just leaving actually,' she started to say, but Pat Johnson put a restraining hand on her arm.

'Oh don't go. Stay and have a drink with me. *Garçon*!' She snapped her fingers imperiously at the waiter. 'What do you drink?' she asked Claire.

'I don't drink in the afternoon,' said Claire, desperately trying to tie the ribbon on her parcel.

'Well, a fruit juice then, or a cup of tea?'

'Well, perhaps . . . an orange juice,' Claire said hesitantly.

'Good.' Pat flashed a bright smile at the waiter. '*Deux jus d'orange, s'il vous plaît.*' Then turning back to Claire she said, 'We've got so much to talk about.'

'Have we?' asked Claire coolly.

'But of course, we've both had the same job, for a start. How do you find the children?'

'They're very sweet.' Claire was deliberately non-committal.

The drinks arrived and Pat took out a silver cigarette case. 'Do you smoke?'

'No thanks.'

Pat lit a cigarette and inhaled deeply. 'And little Philippe—how is his condition?'

'Delicate.' Claire took a sip of her drink. She wasn't going to give anything away.

'Yes, I was so worried about him last year.'

Claire looked at her in amazement. 'Was that why you left him?' she asked quietly.

'Ah that. Well you see you haven't heard all the details.' She calmly continued smoking for several seconds. 'I had no choice you see, not under the circumstances.'

'What circumstances?'

'André asked me to marry him.'

It was like a thunderbolt. Claire caught her breath. 'And . . . what happened?'

'I wasn't sure what I wanted to do. I had to go away and think about it.'

'I see.' Claire's voice trembled. 'And what conclusion did you come to?' she asked icily.

'I haven't made up my mind.' She stubbed out her cigarette in the ashtray.

Claire took another sip of the orange juice. It looked delicious but there was now a bitter taste in her mouth.

'Is that why you've come back?' she asked evenly.

'Oh good heavens, no. I'm just here on holiday. Small world, isn't it?'

She had taken out a silver powder compact, a perfect match with the cigarette case, and was carefully repairing the immaculate mask-like makeup. 'My God, this sea air plays havoc with one's skin, don't you find that?'

'Haven't really thought about it,' said Claire. She drained her glass. 'I must be off.'

'So soon? Ah yes, the working girl. No time to spare. Still if you do get some free time, look me up at the hotel—here's my number,' she said, passing Claire the hotel card. 'It's been lovely to talk to you, goodbye.' She stood up quickly and went off down the road.

Claire picked up the tab as she watched the slim, elegant figure disappear around the corner. Their conversation had left her completely numb. She had suspected something like this but now that it was out in the open she couldn't take it in.

She paid the bill and walked along the road towards the house. Pat's words were in her head all the time. 'André asked me to marry him.' But then what was it André had said?—you mustn't believe everything you hear . . . So what really happened last year?

The next week passed very quickly. Claire enjoyed the mornings at the Mickey Club. Patrick and his friends were always fun to be with. She went out with them on a couple of evenings. Madame Thiret now insisted that Claire have some free time each day. It seemed as if she couldn't do enough to make Claire happy.

On the evening she was due to return to Paris, Claire was having dinner with Madame Thiret when the old lady looked up and said quietly, 'I do hope you stay with the family, my dear. I think you're very good for the children.'

Claire was at a loss for words, it seemed the ultimate accolade in this sombre household. What a difference in attitude the old lady now had towards her. Two weeks ago she had felt like an intruder, now she was a trusted friend.

'You will take great care of the children in Paris, won't you. They're very precious to me. And if ever things are getting too much . . .' she hesitated, 'I mean, Madame Hélène is not the most ideal mother, she has her career to occupy her . . . bring the children back here. You're always welcome.'

'Thank you madame.' Claire felt that words were inadequate to express her gratitude.

Later, as she packed her suitcase in the cool

bedroom overlooking the sea, she thought about the old lady's words. It was so good to feel accepted. She would certainly come back here one day, but at the moment all she wanted to do was to get away . . . back to Paris. It would be marvellous to see the bright lights again.

She tossed the last garment into her suitcase and sat down on the lid. When it was fastened she crossed over to the window and looked out across the bay. The moon was glinting on the water just as it had on her first evening, two weeks ago.

Two weeks . . . it seemed like a lifetime—so much had happened.

Yes, I'll come back here when I can, she thought. I love this house now but there's something I don't understand. She closed the window and, climbing between the cool sheets, she fell asleep listening to the sound of the waves.

Next morning they left early as Henri wanted to get back to Paris before the afternoon rush hour. Claire had asked Madame Thiret if they could take a picnic, so at lunchtime Henri pulled the car off the road into a field.

As Claire unpacked the food she couldn't help thinking about the last time she had looked into this now familiar picnic hamper, that day on the desert island—surely it had been a desert island. A non-existent desert island, cut off from reality.

They reached the outskirts of Paris in mid-afternoon. Already the traffic was beginning to build up to the evening climax, but Henri drove skilfully along the *périphérique* and through the Bois de Boulogne, reaching the relative peace of the Boulevard before the roads became too congested.

The lift climbed up to the penthouse suite and Claire found her spirits soaring with it. She had forgotten just how luxurious everything was. It was a striking contrast to the stark simplicity of the house at Arcachon.

Marie greeted them warmly as they stepped from the lift. She poured out a torrent of voluble colloquial French, some of which Claire had difficulty in understanding, but she gathered that Marie was delighted to see them all again and that Madame Flament was due to return in a couple of days.

'I will take care of the children this evening,' she continued, still in the same rapid French. 'You must be very tired.'

'Thank you Marie. Yes I would like a break right now but I'll come along to the nursery later.'

Marie smiled and started off down the corridor with the children.

Claire made her way to her room. She had a long luxurious bath, then after putting on a cool cotton dress she went along to the nursery.

Opening the door of Philippe's room she was confronted by a tall figure in an immaculate dark suit bending over the bed. She crossed the room, but André continued his careful examination of the tiny figure. After several minutes he raised himself to his full height and looked down at Claire.

'I've arranged to have Philippe admitted tomorrow for tests.'

Claire looked anxiously at the small boy who was wriggling to a sitting position.

'It's all right,' said André. 'I've explained what's happening to Philippe.'

Philippe reached out a small hand and said to Claire, 'Will you come with me?'

'Yes, of course . . . that is—' Claire looked questioningly at André.

'Yes I think that's a good idea. Now where's that maid? Marie!' he called.

'*Oui*, monsieur.' The maid came hurrying in to the room.

'You can serve the children's supper now. If you need us we shall be in the drawing-room.'

Claire stiffened as she felt him take hold of her arm and steer her towards the door.

'Come and have an aperitif before dinner,' he was saying.

He's so very sure of himself, this man, she thought. He can behave as he likes and everyone comes running. Supposing I were to say that I was going to spend the evening in my room. But she was already walking along the corridor, powerless to evade the strong grip on her arm.

She felt like a robot as he led her through the wide doors of the drawing-room towards the comfortable sofa.

'Now, what will you have to drink?' the imperious voice was asking.

Claire surprised herself by replying, 'A gin and tonic.'

'A gin and tonic?' he echoed enquiringly. 'I didn't know you drank gin and tonic.'

'I don't.' Suddenly she laughed and the ice was broken. 'I just feel like trying something different.'

'Yes, of course. *Un gin tonic pour* madame. *Voilà,*' He handed her a crystal glass with a mock flourish.

She took a sip and pulled a face.

André smiled. 'Not what you expected, eh?'

'No, not really. Nothing ever is . . .' Her voice trailed away.

He looked at her quizzically but she didn't elaborate.

'Did you enjoy your last few days at Arcachon?' he asked, moving across the room to sit beside her.

'Yes, very much,' she said quietly.

'Anything exciting happen after I'd gone?'

'Not really . . . Oh, yes. I met Pat Johnson one day.' She was watching him out of the corner of her eye, but he betrayed no emotion. 'We had a drink together.'

'How nice for you.' There was a definite hint of sarcasm in his tone. 'And a long gossip, I shouldn't wonder,' he added.

He was waiting for her to tell him more but she simply smiled and quietly sipped her drink. She wasn't going to give anything away. It was his problem, not hers.

A maid announced that dinner was served and

they went into the elegant dining-room. André sat at the head of the table, with Claire on his right-hand side. What a difference from that first evening when he had completely ignored her. This time he was very attentive throughout the meal, making sure that she enjoyed everything.

They started with fresh asparagus, followed by *poulet basque*, which was delicious chicken in a wine sauce. There was some excellent cheese and then they had strawberries and cream. Claire found that she was beginning to enjoy the French habit of serving the cheese before the dessert. André was generous with the wine and tried, on several occasions, to top up her wine glass but she was careful not to drink too much, remembering the last time they had drunk champagne together. It seemed so long ago now. She put her hand over her wine glass and shook her head as André lifted the wine bottle yet again.

'What's the matter with you tonight? You've hardly drunk anything.' The dark eyes were looking into hers, too close for comfort. She turned away.

'I want to keep a clear head,' she answered lightly.

He shrugged and put the bottle down on the table. 'Maybe you think I'm trying to get you drunk, so I can take advantage of you.' He was grinning broadly, a boyish, wicked grin, which made him look devastatingly handsome.

'I suppose you think that's funny,' she said drily.

'It was meant to be, my little kitten,' he said softly and stretched out his hand to touch her hair. She recoiled as if he were going to strike her.

'Oh come now, I wasn't going to hurt you,' he smiled gently. 'I simply wanted to touch the spun silk of your hair.' As he was speaking he leaned over and placed his arm gently around her shoulders. Claire remained absolutely still as he ran his fingers through her hair.

'Mm, it's so soft,' he murmured as he leaned his head towards her. Before she realised it the dark hair was touching hers and his lips were on her cheek. As if drawn by some unseen force she turned to look into his eyes and his lips moved over hers in a long lingering kiss. She felt weak and helpless, unable to resist the spell which was holding her to him. He pulled her towards him and she responded willingly, longing for the moment to continue. So engrossed were they that neither of them heard the maid come in. It was only when a small voice said,

'Oh . . . *pardon* monsieur!' that Claire broke herself free. The maid had fled from the room in embarrassment and André was shaking with laughter.

Claire ran her hands over her rumpled hair. 'Oh very funny,' she said furiously. 'I'm glad you think it's amusing.'

'Oh come now,' he said, still laughing. 'If you could have seen your face when the maid spoke.'

'I expect she's used to finding you in situations

like this,' said Claire bitterly. 'It must have happened all the time last year.'

He stopped laughing and became deadly serious. 'If that's what you think, then there's nothing more to say,' he said angrily, pushing his chair back from the table. 'I'll see you in the morning. Nine o'clock at the hospital. Henri will take you there. Goodnight.'

He walked quickly out of the room. Claire sat quite still. So she was right, he was still in love with Pat. She was still sitting at the table when the maid came back again.

'Shall I clear the table now, mademoiselle?' she asked politely.

'*Mais oui, bien sûr.*' Claire stood up.

'Will you take coffee in the drawing-room, mademoiselle?'

'No thank you, no coffee tonight.' She went to the nursery to see how the children were. They were both sleeping peacefully so she went along the corridor to her own room. As she got ready for bed, she vowed she would never let André touch her again. He was not going to make use of her while he waited for Pat to make her mind up. The memory of that long, lingering kiss was too disturbing.

CHAPTER SIX

LITTLE Philippe was understandably nervous at breakfast next morning. At first he refused to eat anything and it required all Claire's patience to persuade him to take a few mouthfuls of croissant and jam. Simone, by contrast, was happy and cheerful and sang to herself when she wasn't actually swallowing. Apparently Marie had promised to take her to the zoo for the day while Claire was away with Philippe, and she couldn't wait to set off.

Marie came in to collect her from the breakfast table, beaming all over her face. She adored Simone and loved to be allowed to take her out by herself. Simone jumped down from the table, gave Claire a hasty kiss on the cheek and put her little hand into Marie's.

'*Au revoir* Simone,' said Claire. 'Be a good girl.'

'*Ne vous inquiétez pas*, mademoiselle,' smiled Marie. 'She will be all right with me for the day.' She bent down and patted Philippe gently on the head as she said goodbye to the little boy.

Simone threw her arms round her brother's neck. '*Au revoir*, Philippe,' she said.

Philippe tried to smile bravely but still appeared miserable as he muttered '*Au revoir*, Simone.'

The little girl skipped happily out of the room. Claire decided Philippe was not going to eat any more breakfast, so she helped him down from the table and took him to his room. The small case, with his pyjamas and a few of his favourite toys, was sitting on the bed where Marie had put it, ready packed.

Philippe burst into tears when he saw it. 'I don't want to go, I don't want to leave you,' he said, clinging frantically to Claire.

'Now now, come along, be a brave boy,' Claire pulled the little boy on to her lap and tried to soothe him, 'Uncle André wants you to get better, so he has to find out as much as he can about what's going on inside you.'

Philippe had stopped crying now and was listening to Claire.

'You see, your body is like a car engine. Just like this one,' she continued, picking up one of his toy cars. 'When it's working perfectly, it runs along without any trouble but if one little thing goes wrong it has to be put right. Now, Uncle André thinks that a small part of your body engine isn't working properly, so he's going to test it and then he'll know how to put it right. Don't you think that's a good idea, Philippe?'

'Yes.' The little boy was thoughtful for a few seconds, then he said, 'Uncle André is very clever, isn't he?'

'Yes, he's a very good doctor.'

'I'm glad he's going to make me better. Then I'll be able to run and jump like Simone, won't I?' The little boy was smiling now.

'Yes, of course you will.' Claire gave him a hug. 'Come on now, let's get ready. Henri will be waiting for us.'

Philippe ran into the bathroom and brushed his teeth and washed his hands and face, needing very little help from Claire.

Soon they were going down in the lift to the underground car-park where Henri was waiting for them. He took the small case and put it in the boot, while Claire and Philippe climbed into the back seat, then revving up the engine he drove quickly out through the automatic doors and along the Boulevard to the Arc de Triomphe.

The traffic there was utterly congested, Claire had never seen anything like it. The roundabout which encircled the Arc de Triomphe was jammed solid with cars which were coming in from every direction. Henri seemed to be driving impossibly fast, she closed her eyes as they went into the mass of cars and, unbelievably, when she opened them they were out on the other side and driving down the Champs-Elysées.

'I don't think I should like to drive here myself,' she said to Henri.

'Oh, one gets used to it.' Henri smiled confidently, as he weaved the car expertly in and out of the three lanes of traffic.

They were coming to another roundabout which was surrounded by beautiful fountains, she remembered walking past it with Robert on her first evening in Paris. Turning to Philippe she said, 'See the beautiful fountains, Philippe?'

He looked out and nodded unenthusiastically.

Henri said, '*C'est le Rond Point des Champs-Elysées.*'

The car continued down to the Place de la Concorde and Claire marvelled at the beauty of the large square, and the apparent ease with which Henri negotiated the endless traffic. In the centre she could see a tall beautiful monument which she pointed out to Philippe, trying desperately to keep his spirits up.

'That's the obelisk,' said Henri helpfully. 'It's a very ancient monument, given to France by the Egyptians during the last century.'

Claire had succeeded in getting Philippe interested in what was going on and he now pointed outside, calling out, 'See the big boat on the water.'

They were driving along the side of the River Seine where the huge pleasure boats sail up and down. Soon they crossed the Pont Notre Dame to the Île de la Cité, the most ancient part of Paris. Henri pulled up in front of the Hôtel Dieu hospital and helped Claire and Philippe to get out of the car.

'Shall I wait for you, mademoiselle?' he said.

'No thank you, Henri. I don't know how long I'm going to be.'

'Very good mademoiselle.' Henri took the small case out of the boot and gave it to Claire, who was holding Philippe's hand firmly in hers. They said goodbye to Henri and started to mount the impressive staircase at the entrance.

Claire was so busy helping Philippe to climb each step, that she had not noticed the tall figure standing at the top.

'You're late,' said a deep masculine voice.

Raising her eyes, she saw André impatiently tapping his foot on the top step.

'I said nine o'clock and it's now five past,' he said severely. 'What kept you?'

In spite of his coldness towards her, Claire could not help admiring his appearance, the impeccable dark grey suit, the expensive shirt and tie. He looked every inch the successful consultant. Even so she was annoyed at the way he had received her and found difficulty in composing her reply.

Taking a deep breath she said quietly, 'I'm sorry we're late, but the traffic was terrible.'

'Traffic, traffic—I know all about the traffic. I came through it myself and I was here an hour ago,' he snapped.

'Yes but . . .' she started, and then stopped when she saw the forbidding look on his face. The dark hostile eyes seemed to pierce inside her. She turned away and bent down to pick up little Philippe, who was tired after climbing the stairs.

'*Bonjour* Philippe,' he said gently. '*Ça va mon petit chou*?'

'*Oui, ça va.*' Philippe smiled at his uncle. 'You're going to make me better, aren't you?'

André smiled. 'We're going to try.' He started to walk briskly along the corridor, carrying Philippe as if he were a tiny bird in his strong arms. Claire followed along behind them, feeling unwanted and forgotten.

'This is a very good hospital,' André was saying to Philippe. 'The building is historically very famous. There has been a hospital here for hundreds of years but it's been rebuilt several times.'

Claire looked at the stone pillars and the high ceiling of the corridor. It was a very awe-inspiring place, rather like a great cathedral, she thought.

'But although it's a historical building it has some of the finest equipment in the world,' André continued his explanation.

'And the best doctor,' said Philippe as he snuggled his head against his uncle's shoulder.

André appeared to be smiling to himself as Claire caught up with them but his face was stern when he turned to face her. 'There's no need for you to stay, Nurse,' he said. 'The hospital is fully staffed.'

'But I thought Philippe might need me here . . .' she began.

'He will be in good hands,' André said brusquely. 'You may take the day off. Here we are.' He stopped in front of the door to the childrens' ward.

'*Au revoir*, Philippe,' said Claire.

The small head reached up and she bent to give him a kiss. As she did so her hair brushed against the dark suit and she smelt the now-familiar, utterly disturbing, expensive after-shave. She lifted her head quickly and retraced her steps hurriedly down the corridor, not daring to see if those mocking eyes were watching her. Hot tears were pricking her eyelids and she willed them not to fall until she was outside the building.

It was warm when she emerged from the sombre building and she blinked away the tears. As her eyes accustomed themselves to the bright sunlight, she found she was in the Place du Parvis. Across the ancient square she could see the majestic towers of Notre Dame. A small café nestled amongst the buildings near the Cathedral and she walked across and went inside, sinking thankfully on to a chair at a table in a dark corner.

'Mademoiselle *désire*?' the waiter hovered beside her.

'*Un café, s'il vous plaît.*' It was at times like this she wished she smoked, but when the strong black coffee arrived she felt some of her composure returning. What an obnoxious man André could be, how could she have allowed herself to be taken in by him, even for a few moments? She took another sip of the coffee and started to feel better.

A whole day off—and in Paris, she thought. Mustn't waste it. I must see something of Paris but where shall I start. Perhaps I'll buy a guide book—no, I'll ring Robert.

She drained her coffee, stood up decisively and went over to the counter before she could change her mind.

'Is there a telephone here?' she asked the waiter, who was washing glasses behind the bar.

'*Oui*, mademoiselle, but only for calls inside Paris.'

Claire nodded.

'You must buy *un jeton* to put into the telephone. It doesn't take francs.' He went over to the till. 'Here you are.'

Claire paid for the metal disc and for the coffee, then went down into the basement to the telephone. She found Robert's number in her diary and dialled it.

It rang several times and she was on the point of replacing the receiver when he answered. 'Hello.' He sounded breathless, as if he'd been running.

'Robert. It's Claire, I was beginning to think you were out.'

'I almost was, I was on my way out when I heard the phone ring. I've got to be at the language school at ten.'

'Oh,' she felt disappointed. 'I was hoping you might be able to show me round Paris.'

'Aren't you working?'

'Not today—I've got the day off.'

'How marvellous. Look, I've got a lesson from ten to eleven and then I'll arrange to free myself for the rest of the day.'

'Can you do that?'

'Sure—we only get paid for the hours we work. There's always someone willing to take on the extra lessons—and the extra money.'

'But can you afford it?'

'My dear girl, I can afford anything where you're concerned.' He laughed happily. 'Where are you, by the way?'

'I'm in a café near Notre Dame.'

'Fine. You can look round Notre Dame and I'll meet you outside at about eleven-thirty. Look, I must dash—is that OK?'

'Yes, I'll be there—and thanks Robert.'

'My pleasure—see you soon.'

She put the phone down and went back upstairs into the cafe. She smiled at the waiter and he smiled back. It was going to be a good day after all.

She crossed the square and went into Notre Dame. After the warm, bright sunlight it seemed dark and cold but the light from the numerous candles gave it a sombre glow. Claire felt an enormous feeling of peace descend upon her as she stood looking up at the huge dome. For centuries people had worshipped here, it was awe-inspiring; she felt very small and insignificant as she crept quietly into one of the back pews and knelt down to say a short prayer.

Rising from her knees she sat quietly in the pew for a few minutes, drinking in the atmosphere. Tourists of all nationalities were thronging the aisles, discussing the various aspects of the architecture, the statues, the stone pillars, the altars. Claire could hear a smattering of English here and there, some obvious Germans passed by and the inevitable French tourists from the provinces, here for a day trip or a few days' holiday. Up in the high loft someone was practising the organ, the strains of Bach's Toccata and Fugue filled the air majestically. After several minutes, Claire stood up and walked down the central aisle to the main altar, where she stood for a while, mesmerized by its magnificence. A service was about to begin and the central part of the cathedral was being cleared, so Claire made her way to the entrance of the North Tower. She bought a ticket and climbed the rough stone stairs until she could look out across the Ile de la Cité and the whole of Paris, stretching away into the distance. She crossed to the South Tower before going back down to the main body of Notre Dame.

The service was in full progress by this time and the congregation were joining in the prayers and chants. Claire sat down once more, near the back, and listened and watched. It was very impressive to see and hear.

When the service was over she walked out into the bright sunlight to find that it was almost time to meet Robert. She hovered in the entrance for a few minutes and then saw him crossing the square, his faint, curly hair flapping over his face. He was wearing a pair of faded jeans and a tee-shirt. What a contrast with the distinguished style of the man she had left earlier this morning.

He waved happily when he saw Claire at the front of Notre Dame and she went to meet him. He clasped her by the hands and leaned forward to kiss her on the cheek.

'What a lovely surprise,' he said. 'When did you get back from Arcachon?'

'Yesterday.'

'Well, I'm honoured you should ring me on the first day. What happened? Is the delectable doctor working or something?'

'Oh, don't be silly, Robert,' she said lightly. 'He's only my employer. Besides he's an arrogant so-and-so. I couldn't possibly go out with him.'

'Unless he asked you . . .' Robert started, but Claire stopped him.

'Look Robert, I don't want to talk about him.'

'Of course not. I'm sorry, Claire. Here we are in gay Paree and a whole day to ourselves. What do you want to see first?'

'Well I don't know—you're the expert. What is there to see? I've done the Eiffel Tower, by the way,' she said laughingly. 'I came on a trip from school a few years ago.'

'OK. How about Montmartre?'

'Oh yes. Isn't that where all the artists live?'

'Used to. Now it's becoming rather touristy but you still get lots of artists painting and selling their pictures in the Place du Tertre. Anyway we must see the Sacré Coeur while we're up there. Come on we'll get the metro.'

They were soon rattling along in the underground train towards the north of Paris. After a couple of changes they reached Anvers station and started walking up the steep Rue de Steinkerque. Claire was fascinated by the shops and boutiques on either side of the narrow street and insisted on wandering in and out to look at the variety of goods on display—shoes, material and all kinds of souvenirs.

The whole area was bustling with noise and activity. At the top of the street they could see the dome of the Sacré Coeur with its tall spire pointing up into the blue sky. They climbed up through the gardens in front of it and stood for a few minutes on the steps, admiring the view. Foreign street traders displayed their goods on the paths, there were leather bags and hats and the inevitable souvenirs. Robert haggled with an African trader until he brought the price of a leather hat within his reach. Having bought it, he stuck it jauntily on his head, grinning amiably at Claire.

'Would you like one, madame?' asked the trader.

'No thanks,' Claire smiled at him. 'Not really my style.'

'But I give you very good price, madame.'

'No thanks,' she said firmly and walked towards the entrance of the cathedral. 'Come on Robert. Let's get on with our guided tour.'

Robert took her by the hand and together they went into the Sacré Coeur. Claire thought the interior of the building was gentler and not so austere as Notre Dame. Again it was lit by many candles and the effect was an overall fairyland atmosphere.

They climbed the stairs up to the dome and gazed

out over the panorama of Paris spread out before them. As they walked round the gallery of the dome, they saw the bleak new industrial area of La Défense to the west, and the older, more picturesque areas of Paris to the south, in the distance was the river, and on the other side of it they could see the Eiffel Tower.

'That was marvellous,' she enthused as they went back down the steps and out once more into the sunshine. 'I wouldn't have missed it for anything.'

'Yes, it's certainly worth the climb. Now what about lunch? Are you hungry?'

'Starving,' she laughed.

'Good. I know just the place. Cheap and cheerful, but full of character. *Très Parisien*.' He laughed and took her hand as they walked side by side along the cobbled street to the Place du Tertre.

'Oh, see the artists,' Claire said excitedly. 'We must stop and have a look.'

'Later,' said Robert. 'We'll come back, lunch first. This place we're going to gets very crowded. We'll never get a table if we don't hurry.'

He rushed her along the edge of the Place du Tertre, down a narrow street and into a small restaurant with bright red and white checked tablecloths. Candles were dripping their wax down the sides of bottles and an accordionist was playing in the corner.

Every table seemed to be full, mostly young people, students or artists; everyone appeared to be enjoying themselves. Claire felt herself invigorated by the lively atmosphere. A smiling waiter beckoned them to follow him to a tiny table, squashed in between the accordion player and the kitchen. They squeezed into the narrow space and the waiter produced the menu.

'Oh, *ça n'est pas nécessaire*,' said Robert. 'We'll have the *plat du jour*. It's always good. What is it, by the way?'

'Today we have *poulet rôti,* monsieur.'

'*Très bien*,' said Robert. '*Deux, s'il vous plait*, and a carafe of the house red wine.'

'*Oui* monsieur.' The waiter vanished into the kitchen.

Claire felt slightly deflated. She would have liked to have chosen from the menu, but if Robert wanted them to have the dish of the day, she wouldn't argue. It was always the most economical thing to have and she remembered that Robert was actually giving up some of his teaching fees to take her out.

'You must let me pay my share of the bill,' she started to say, but he interrupted her at once.

'Wouldn't dream of it. It's my treat today.' He reached across the table and squeezed her hand. 'I may be slightly impoverished but you're worth every penny—I mean, every franc.' They both laughed.

The accordionist had started to play the cancan and two young couples were trying to dance between the tables, not very successfully, because of the lack of space. A glass fell to the floor with a crash and everyone clapped their hands and cheered.

The waiter brought the wine and filled their glasses. It tasted rough after the vintage wines she had become used to with André, but she suppressed a shudder and smiled at Robert across the table as she raise her glass.

'*Santé.*'

'*Santé*,' he replied, clinking his glass against hers.

The roast chicken, when it arrived, was delicious, garnished with herbs and tiny French fries. Robert ordered ice-cream to follow and attentively topped up Claire's glass every time she took a drink. The wine didn't taste too bad after the first glass, she felt quite merry by the end of the meal, and began to think what a good friend Robert was.

The waiter cleared the table and brought coffee.

'Would you like a cognac?' said Robert.

'Good heavens, no. I feel like dancing on the table already,' she laughed.

'Good, that's the way I like you. You look much happier than when we first met this morning. What was the matter, don't you like your job?'

'It's difficult to adapt to private nursing, it's neither one thing nor the other—and it can be lonely you know. I miss the comradeship of hospital life,' she said, feeling relieved to have been able to tell someone at least part of the problem.

'Well there's no need to be lonely here in Paris, because I'm going to give you the time of your life,' Robert said as he reached across the table to squeeze her hand. He paid the bill and stood up. 'Come on, let's go and have a look at the paintings in the square.'

They walked up the street and wandered into the Place du Tertre. It was full of artists displaying their paintings. Some were busily sketching or painting at their easels. One artist approached Robert and said, 'Let me sketch your beautiful lady, monsieur.'

'How much?' said Robert practically.

'Oh, monsieur, for a beautiful lady like yours, I make a special price.'

'How much?' repeated Robert.

The artist named a price. Robert laughed. 'That's far too much.' He started to walk away, the artist followed him.

'For you, monsieur, I take off ten francs,' a special price.'

'OK.' Robert turned round. 'But you'd better make it good.'

Claire stopped still. 'Robert, I don't really want to be sketched.'

'Of course you do. Come on, sit down.'

The artist had drawn up a chair and begun to sketch, while a small crowd was gathering around to watch. Claire felt terribly conspicuous.

'Smile,' Robert was saying and she dutifully smiled, wondering how long the ordeal would last.

After what seemed liked an eternity, the artist ripped the portrait from his sketch pad with a flourish.

'*Voilá,*' he said proudly.

'It's not as beautiful as she is but it'll do,' said Robert grudgingly, handing over the agreed price. 'What do you think of it, Claire?'

She stared at the portrait of herself. In spite of the bright smile there was a sadness about her face.

'It's a good likeness, I think. Thank you,' she said to the artist.

He smiled. 'It's always a pleasure to draw a beautiful young lady. *Au revoir*, madame, *au revoir*, monsieur.'

They wandered through the narrow cobbled streets, down the hill, until they found themselves at the Place de Clichy. They sat in a café for a while drinking coffee and watching the traffic hurtling past.

'There's a concert I want to go to this evening,' said Robert. 'Will you come?'

'Oh I can't stay out this evening. I should be getting back,' Claire said quickly.

'Why?' he sounded impatient.

'Well, I've been out all day, I mean . . . they may need me,' she finished lamely.

'Nonsense, your patient's in hospital, the maid's looking after the other child. What's the problem? Anyway, it's an early evening concert.'

'Well . . . What time does it start?'

'Six o'clock, till about seven thirty. It's a radio broadcast at the Maison de la Radio. You have to queue up three-quaters of an hour before its starts and they give you a free ticket to be part of the studio audience. I often go, it's a young soprano this evening, making her radio debut. I've heard she's very good. Afterwards I'll take you to a delicious *crêperie* I know, and buy you the *crêpe* of your choice. How about that?'

'OK, you're on,' she laughed. 'Let's go.'

They crossed Paris by metro, alighting at Alma Marceau, by the side of the river.

'This is one of my favourite walks in Paris,' said Robert as he took her to the middle of a bridge spanning the Seine. From the middle of the bridge they went down wide steps leading to the narrow island and walked along between the Left and Right Banks of the Seine. It was very peaceful, boats were sailing past and the branches of the trees dipped their leaves into the water.

After a few minutes' walk, Robert pointed out the impressive, circular building of the French Broadcasting House on the Right Bank of the river.

The building looked incongruously new, with its huge plate-glass windows, surrounded as it was by the older buildings of Paris.

The end of the Allée des Cygnes had been shaped into a curve, like the bow of a ship, dominated by the Statue of Liberty.

'This is a direct replica of the one in the United States,' said Robert pointing up at the enormous stone statue. 'When the Americans took the original one over there, they gave this one to France. Beautiful isn't it.'

'Mm.' Claire was gazing out across the water at the end of the Allée.

They were quite alone on this narrow island in the middle of the Seine. The later afternoon sun was casting a glowing red path of sunlight on to the river, and it was falling full on to her face.

'Penny for them,' said Robert, coming up behind her and putting his hand on her waist. 'You look as if you're miles away.'

'No, I'm just enjoying myself. It's been a lovely day, Robert.'

'Not over yet, my precious.' Suddenly he tightened his grip on her waist and pulled her towards him. She could feel the taut muscles of his body flexing, as he pressed himself against her. His mouth came down on hers before she could move away, and her lips were crushed in a long passionate kiss. She willed herself to enjoy it. If only she could feel some of the thrill which had shot through her when André kissed her, but her body felt cold and unresponsive. His hands were starting to move excitedly towards her breasts as she pulled herself away.

'No, Robert, no. Let's not spoil the day.'

He laughed bitterly. 'So it would spoil the day, would it, to behave like a normal couple? How long do we have to keep up the brother and sister act? You might like it, but I don't. You may be able to fool yourself, but you don't fool me. You're in love with that wretched doctor—no, don't deny it,' he shouted angrily, as she began to protest.

'Robert you're wrong. I'm not in love with him. I'm not.' She was shaking with emotion.

'OK, calm down, I'm sorry. Look, let's sit down. We're both getting overheated.' He pulled her gently down on to the cool marble at the foot of the statue. They both sat quietly for a few minutes, watching the changing scene on the river. Then Robert looked at his watch.

'I think we should go,' he said. 'If we're going to get tickets.'

They walked across the Pont de Grenelle to the Maison de la Radio and in through the revolving glass doors. A small queue was already forming in front of the box office and they stood together in awkward silence. Claire was the first to break it.

'I think I'd better ring Marie to see if everything's OK,' she said quietly.

Robert shrugged. 'As you wish,' he said in a flat voice.

Claire went over to the phone kiosk and dialled the Flaments' number. When she got through, Marie gabbled excitedly about their day at the zoo. Simone came to the phone and added her account of the animals which seemed as if it would never end. She managed to get Marie back on the line so that she could ask about Philippe, and was told that she had no further news.

'I'll be back about ten o'clock, Marie. Will you put Simone to bed?'

'*Bien sûr*,' said the maid happily, 'Enjoy yourself mademoiselle.'

Claire could see Robert gesticulating from the

other side of the foyer. 'I'll have to go. *Au revoir*, Marie.'

'*Au revoir*, mademoiselle.'

Robert had got the tickets but he was anxious to get into the studio and find a good seat. They settled themselves in the centre near the front and waited the half-hour until the concert started.

'I think you were hoping they would want you to go back home when you rang, weren't you,' said Robert slyly.

'No, of course I wasn't,' Claire said. It was so maddening to be with someone who kept reading her thoughts. She wished the concert would start so that the evening would be over as quickly as possible.

When the young soprano came on to the stage, however, Claire forgot all her misgivings. She had a superb voice and was obviously very talented. First she sang in French, the Berlioz song cycle, *Les Nuits d'Été*. This was followed by some songs of Villa Lobos in Portuguese. The highlight of the concert, for Claire at any rate, was the final song cycle by Leonard Bernstein, called 'I Hate Music' which was sung in English. It was an interpretation of a young child saying that she hated music, but she loved to sing. It was very amusing and the audience laughed. As Claire joined in, she relaxed again, she turned and smiled at Robert. He took her hand and squeezed it gently.

'Friends?' he asked.

'Friends,' she said, but removed her hand all the same.

When the recital was over they went out into the warm evening and crossed the street to the *crêperie*. This time Claire was allowed to peruse the menu and she chose her own *crêpe*. The thin pancake she ordered was soaked in brandy and tasted delicious.

'How do I get back from here?' she asked Robert, as they finished the *crêpes* and drank their coffee.

'It's a bit difficult by metro from here. I think we'll take a taxi. Blow the expense. I've got to convince you somehow that I love you,' he said in a matter-of-fact tone.

'Oh Robert. Please don't say it.'

'Why not, it's true.'

'Can't we just be good friends?'

'For the moment, yes. But it's a bit of a strain. Come on, let's find that cab.'

They went out into the street, and Robert waved his hand furiously at a passing taxi, which screeched to a halt. Robert grasped her hand in his and Claire held her breath.

'Don't worry, I'm not going to try anything,' he muttered. 'But patience isn't one of my virtues, and I'm only human after all, so don't think I can hold out forever.'

'It's been a most enjoyable day, Robert,' Claire said brightly. 'Thank you very much.'

He didn't reply and she felt relieved when the taxi drew up outside the Flaments' apartment. He opened the door to let her out, kissing her lightly as she squeezed past.

'I'll give you a ring sometime,' she said.

'Yes, do that. Goodbye.'

She took the lift and got out at the penthouse suite. It was very quiet. She went along to the nursery and found Marie in the kitchen.

'Dr Dubois is waiting for you in the drawing-room, mademoiselle,' she said.

Claire's heart was beating wildly as she hurried back along the corridor and into the drawing-room. André was sitting by the open window, smoking a cigar and sipping a glass of cognac. He looked up when she came in.

'Ah, so the wanderer returns,' he said drily.

'Is everything all right with Philippe?' she asked quickly.

'Yes, yes of course. We haven't done much with him today. Just the preliminary cardiac tests. Don't look so worried.'

'I thought something must have happened because you were here.'

'No, I just wanted to see your pretty face again, that's all. I came early, hoping to have dinner with you, but the bird had flown. Have you had dinner, by the way?'

'Sort of,' she said feebly.

'Sort of?' he repeated. 'In France either we have dinner or we don't have dinner. What did you have?'

'*Crépes*,' she said defensively.

'That's not dinner. I suppose you were out with that young boyfriend of yours. You must allow me to take you out to dinner—or better still, how about lunch tomorrow?'

Taken completely off-guard, she opened her mouth to say no, but even as her lips started to move she weakened.

'Y . . . yes . . .' she stammered feebly. 'If Philippe's still in hospital, I shall be free again.'

'Fine. He's having his electrocardiogram in the morning. Meet me at the hospital about noon. I'll take you in to see him and we can have lunch afterwards.'

She was standing awkwardly by the door, not trusting herself to cross the room, but André came towards her. He looked down into her eyes and she turned her head so that he could not see the depth of emotion welling up inside her. She made a move towards the door but his arm restrained her.

'Don't hurry away. I thought we could have a drink together.' His voice was soft and caressing.

'No, I'm going to bed,' she said abruptly, to hide her feelings.

He brushed his hand lightly across her hair, and she shivered at the unexpected contact.

'Goodnight,' he said softly.

'Goodnight,' she said, going quickly through the door before she could change her mind.

CHAPTER SEVEN

SIMONE came bounding into Claire's bedroom early the next morning. The little girl jumped on her bed and planted a kiss on Claire's cheek. For a moment, as she opened her eyes, Claire could not remember where she was, then the events of the previous day came flooding back—Robert's guided tour of Paris, and André's invitation to lunch. She gave Simone a gentle hug.

'Go and get dressed, Simone. I'll come along to the nursery in a few minutes,' she said gently.

'Can I see Philippe today?' the little girl asked.

'No, I'm afraid not, but I'll give him your love when I see him.'

'When are you going to the hospital?' Simone asked.

'This morning,' Claire said.

'Oh.' The little girl looked dejected. 'I hoped you were going to play with me today,' she said wistfully. 'I didn't see you yesterday when I came back from the zoo.'

'I've got time to play with you before I go,' said Claire. 'Go and get dressed and I'll take you for a walk after breakfast. Where would you like to go?'

'Oh, can we go to the Ranelagh Gardens—it's not far—and they've got swings and slides and donkey rides.' It all came tumbling out in a jumble of incoherent French, but Claire managed to decipher most of it.

'All right,' she smiled. 'Run along, I'll be with you soon.'

The little girl danced happily out of the room, leaving Claire to dress in peace.

Immediately after breakfast they walked down the Boulevard to the Ranelagh Gardens. It was still early in the day, so there were few people about when they reached the swings and slides. The donkeys were still sleepily cropping the grass, and their keeper seemed in no hurry to harness them.

'You can have a ride later, Simone,' said Claire. 'Come on, I'll push you on the swings.'

The little girl happily jumped on to a swing, singing to herself as she was pushed to and fro. Next she wanted to go on the slide, so Claire hovered anxiously as the tiny figure climbed up the steps and hurtled down the slippery slope. After this, they made their way to the sand-pit and Claire produced Simone's bucket and spade from her bag. This meant that she was able to sit down on one of the seats while she watched the little girl playing happily with the other children who had started to drift in, accompanied by their mothers or nannies.

The time passed quickly, and when Claire glanced at her watch she saw that they would have to go if she were to get to the hospital by noon. Mustn't keep the great man waiting.

'Simone,' she called gently. 'Time to go now.'

The little girl pulled a face in dismay. 'Oh not yet!

I haven't had my donkey-ride.'

This was true. Claire had forgotten all about the donkeys.

'I tell you what, we'll come back this afternoon. OK?' She knew as soon as she'd said it that she might regret it, but a promise was a promise, especially to a child.

Simone smiled happily and, picking up her bucket and spade, she trotted over to Claire. 'Will you come back to me as soon as you've seen Philippe?' she asked.

'Well . . . er. . . . no—not immediately. I've promised to have lunch with Uncle André, but I'll come back as soon as I can.'

The little girl put her sandy hand trustingly into Claire's and they walked back through the gardens. Simone stopped as they passed the donkeys.

'Can I stroke one?' she asked the attendant.

'*Bien sûr, chérie.*' The swarthy-skinned young man flashed a pearly-white smile at the little girl. He lifted her up so that she could stroke the donkey's neck. 'Do you want a ride, my pet?'

'We haven't time, just now,' put in Claire quickly. 'But we'll come back this afternoon.'

'Which donkey would you like to ride?' persisted the young man.

'Oo, this one—he's lovely,' said Simone, patting the donkey's nose.

'I'll save him for you, *chérie*.'

'*Merci*,' said Claire. 'Now we really must go. *Au revoir*.'

'*Au revoir* mesdemoiselles. *A bientôt.*'

Claire hurried away, holding Simone firmly by the hand.

'What a lovely donkey,' Simone said as they walked out of the gardens.

'Yes, isn't he. Come along Simone, can you walk a little quicker? I don't want to be late.'

They crossed at the zebra crossing, and cut through a narrow street into the Boulevard. Simone was starting to drag on Claire's hand, so she picked her up and carried her the last few yards.

Marie was waiting for them as they came out of the lift. She smiled and lifted Simone into her arms. 'I heard the lift coming and thought it was you, mademoiselle. Would you like some coffee?'

'No thanks, I haven't time, Marie. If you'll just take care of Simone until I get back, that will be fine.'

'Certainly, mademoiselle. Come along, Simone. We'll go and have a drink in the nursery,' the maid said.

'*Au revoir,*' Simone said the Claire. 'You won't forget the donkeys will you?'

'Donkeys?' asked Marie.

'I've promised Simone she may have a donkey ride this afternoon,' said Claire. 'So I'll be back soon after lunch.'

'Fine, I'll have her ready for you. *Au revoir*, mademoiselle.' The maid went off down the corridor, carrying Simone in her arms.

Claire hurried to her room and pulled off her

cotton dress. What should she wear? It was sure to be a smart restaurant. She cast her eyes over her limited wardrobe. If only I'd bought a new dress in Arcachon, instead of spending my money on that expensive bikini, she thought. Now what have I got that's remotely suitable? There was her cream silk suit, she had brought it 'just in case', having always felt slightly overdressed in it. She remembered having bought it for someone's wedding. Oh, well, this was Paris after all. She put on her grandmother's silver necklace, the clasp always defeated her initially and as she struggled with it, she smiled to herself, half-expecting the sensitive hands of the surgeon to come upon her from behind, as they had done once before.

At last she was ready. She looked in the mirror and smiled. She looked truly elegant—perhaps too elegant? If I put on a hat and gloves, I could go to a Royal Garden Party, she thought wryly. Oh well, there's no time to change now.

She picked up her one and only bag, which definitely didn't go with the outfit and hurried along to the lift. She pressed the button, it seemed ages before the doors finally opened.

Down they went . . . slowly, slowly—or so it seemed. She glanced nervously at her watch. I'll never make it, she thought.

Across the foyer and out into the morning sunshine. The traffic was roaring past at a furious pace. How do you stop a taxi in Paris? she wondered as she saw one in the middle lane. Hopefully she raised her hand and waved. The taxi swerved across in front of two cars and screeched to a halt at the kerb-side. Claire climbed in and sank thankfully on to the back seat.

'Hôpital Hôtel Dieu, *s'il vous plaît,*' she said breathlessly to the driver.

He nodded and roared off at a furious pace towards the Arc de Triomphe. Claire closed her eyes until they were safely at the other side and hurtling down the Champs-Elysées. She glanced at her watch—ten minutes to twelve.

Oh please hurry, she said to herself. Let me get there on time today.

The taxi tore round the Place de la Concorde, along the river bank, across to the Île de la Cité, and came to a halt outside the hospital.

Two minutes to twelve. Claire paid the driver and looked up the entrance staircase. There was no one at the top.

Good, she thought. I've made it. She took a deep breath and walked leisurely up the stairs. As if by magic the tall handsome figure of André Dubois appeared as she reached the top step.

'That was good timing,' he said approvingly, as he took her arm and steered her along the corridor. 'Philippe is longing to see you.'

'How is he?' she asked.

'It's too soon to co-ordinate all the results of the tests. I'll be able to give you a full report tomorrow, when I bring him home,' he said briefly. 'He's settled in very well at the hospital. I wanted him to get used to the place, because we shall have to operate within the next few months, I think.'

They had reached the childrens' ward and André pushed open the swing door to allow Claire to go through. Once inside she felt that she was most unsuitably dressed for hospital visiting. How she wished she could somehow slide inside her comfortable nurse's uniform and hide the long blonde hair under a starched white cap.

The ward sister came gliding noiselessly towards them.

'This is Nurse Baxter, Sister,' said André. 'She will be in charge of Philippe's nursing care when he goes home.'

Sister gave her a friendly smile as André strode purposefully across to Philippe's bed. The little boy was propped up on pillows, looking pale and tired, but his face lit up when he saw Claire. She bent to kiss him gently and his little hand took hold of hers.

'I'm glad you came,' he said. 'I've missed you, but I've been a good boy—haven't I, Uncle André.'

'Oh, very good, so good that you can go home tomorrow,' smiled André.

'Oo, thank you,' the little boy said happily.

Claire sat down on a chair at Philippe's bedside. It was good to be back in hospital. She felt this was where she belonged. Yes, she would finish her contract with the Flament family and then go back to nursing in England. There was no point in staying around in France . . .

'I like your pretty dress.' Philippe's little voice

cut in on her thoughts. 'Are you going to a wedding?'

Out of the mouths of babes and sucklings! she thought.

'No Philippe,' she said, out loud. 'I'm not going to a wedding.'

André was trying to suppress a smile. 'Nurse Baxter is coming out for lunch with me,' he said. 'I think she's put her best dress on for the occasion.'

Claire wanted to sink through the floor in embarrassment. What a poor little country cousin he must think her. Pat Johnson would have known what to wear. She glanced up at the self-assured figure beside her, but his eyes gave nothing away.

They stayed for several minutes with Philippe before André said, 'We've got to go now, Philippe, but I'll come back later this afternoon to see you.'

The little boy smiled and waved bravely as Claire and André went out through the door.

'He needs building up, he's too weak at the moment,' said André, as they went down the corridor. 'When he comes out, I want you to devote your whole attention to him until we operate.'

Claire's interest was raised. At least she would have an important part to play during the next few months, and after that, back to England.

They went out into the front of the hospital and crossed the Place du Parvis. 'There's no point in taking the car, it's much too difficult to park around here at this time of day,' said André. 'It's not far.'

They had started to cross the Pont de Notre

Dame when André took her arm. Claire walked stiffly by his side. He's only being polite, she thought. When they reached the Left Bank they walked through a maze of narrow streets until they came to a picturesque old building, set back from a cobbled courtyard. André led her inside. When her eyes became accustomed to the subdued lighting of the interior, she saw that they were in a very exclusive restaurant, the sort of place she had always dreamed of, but never thought she would be able to afford. A waiter was showing them to a table and Claire took a deep breath as she followed André. The waiter held out her chair.

'Madame,' he said and waited until she had slid herself inexpertly on to it. She placed her shabby bag under the table, where it would be as inconspicuous as possible. She looked up and saw that André was watching her.

'Don't worry,' he whispered in English. 'You look lovely.'

She smiled shyly and glanced at the menu which the waiter had placed in her hand. She could hear André ordering the aperitifs and was glad he hadn't consulted her about what she wanted. Her eyes wandered helplessly over the menu, it was more like a book of *haute cuisine*; there were several pages and Claire wondered where she should begin and how many courses they were going to have.

'Would you like me to order for you?' asked André, again in English.

'Oh, yes please. I really don't know where to start,' she blurted out.

'Well, start by taking a sip of your aperitif,' he said kindly. 'And leave the rest to me.'

Claire picked up the delicate crystal glass and took a sip of the clear green liquid while André conferred with the waiter about the menu. When he had finished, Claire asked,

'What do you call this?'

'It's Crème de Menthe with crushed ice. Do you like it?'

'Yes, it's very refreshing.' She started to unwind, and glanced round at the other tables.

This is an entirely different place from the cheap-and-cheerful restaurant of yesterday, she thought. She took another sip of her aperitif. Yes, I could actually enjoy this, if only I were a little more suitably dressed. She looked at the woman on the next table who simply exuded Paris chic from her exquisitely coiffured hair to her immaculate manicure. Claire glanced down at her own nails and carefully curled them into the palms of her hands. She could actually see small grains of sand underneath her nails from the sand-pit.

'How many times have you been to Paris?' André was saying in a polite conversational voice.

'Only once. I came for a few days with a school party when I was about twelve.'

'Good heavens, but you speak such good French. I thought you must have been here many times before.' He sounded surprised.

'No, my grandmother was French, but she died when I was five. She used to talk to me in French when I was small and I found I could understand her easily. It all came back to me when we learned French at school.'

'Ah, your grandmother . . . the one who gave you the beautiful necklace.'

'Yes,' Claire's hand crept automatically to finger it at her throat.'

'It's very beautiful,' he said. 'Quite the most beautiful necklace in the room,' he added.

Oh what a lovely thing to say, thought Claire. Just when I need a boost to my morale. She sat up a little straighter in her chair. Perhaps this suit isn't so bad after all.

The waiter was placing a dish of oysters in front of her. She watched anxiously to see how André would open them and then tried to copy him. The waiter poured some cold white wine into her glass. As she raised it to her lips, her eyes met André's across the table. He was smiling at her.

'Do you like this place?' he asked.

'Yes, it's . . . er . . . different,' she said.

'Different?' he queried.

'Different from any restaurant I've ever been in—not a bit like the one I was in yesterday,' she added, smiling in amusement as she remembered the couple dancing the cancan between the tables.

'Ah, yes, you were out with your boyfriend weren't you.' The smile had gone from his face. 'I'd quite forgotten. And how is the young man?'

'He's very well, enjoying life in Paris,' she said brightly, concentrating her efforts on the final oyster.

'And still enjoying number one place in your affections.'

It was a statement, not a question.

'No, of course not. We're just good friends.' Then changing the subject quickly she said, 'I've never eaten oysters before. They were declicious.'

He smiled 'I'm glad you approve of my choice. Do you like pheasant by the way?'

'I'm not sure. Maybe I do,' was her naïve reply.

He laughed. 'Well I'm sure you'll like the way they serve it here.'

He was quite right, Claire found the succulent pheasant tasted delicious.

'I honestly can't eat anything else,' she whispered to André after the pheasant course. 'I'm not used to having a large lunch.'

'That's all right,' he said. 'I'll take a little cheese and then we'll just have coffee.'

They lingered over their coffee at the end of the meal. There was a subdued murmur of conversation and a subtle hint of music somewhere in the background. The whole ambience had a mellowing effect on Claire and she knew she could get to like this sort of place if given time. She looked across at the handsome figure seated opposite her and she experienced that warm sensation she was trying to fight against. What a pity he's so involved with another woman, she thought.

'What are you thinking?' he asked gently.

'Oh . . . nothing much,' she answered lightly. Better not to spoil the atmosphere with any prying questions.

She looked into those dark, expressive eyes and knew that if they were alone she would find great difficulty in controlling her seething emotions.

'Would you like to come back to my apartment for a small cognac? I don't have to be back in hospital until later this afternoon.'

Claire heard the smooth seductive voice across the table as if in a dream. Yes, oh yes, her heart whispered, but her mundane reply gave no hint of the turmoil that was going on inside her. 'I've promised to take Simone for a donkey ride.'

He threw back his head and laughed. 'But my dear child, Simone will wait for you. I've got lots of important things to do at the hospital this afternoon, but in France we take a leisurely lunch. We don't hurry things. If you come back to my apartment, you can taste one of the finest cognacs in France. It's all part of your education you know. After all, I promised to teach you about wines,' he added, giving her his mischievous boyish grin.

She smiled. 'You can be very persuasive, André.'

'I know,' he laughed lightly.

They went out into the courtyard, where the bright afternoon sunlight was filtering down between the ancient buildings. A taxi was waiting for them. André must have ordered it, she thought, enjoying the feeling of complete luxury which enveloped her. She climbed into the back seat and André slid in beside her, giving brief instructions to the driver.

They roared off through the narrow streets, across the Pont d'Arcole to the Right Bank and along the Rue de Rivoli with its picturesque arcades. Somewhere near the Palais Royal, the taxi turned off into a tree-lined avenue and pulled up in front of a large, impressive old house. André paid the driver and led Claire up the front steps.

'Here is my apartment,' he said, with obvious pride. 'It's an oasis of calm in this busy city. I like to return here to relax in the middle of the day whenever I can. Sometimes I take a siesta.' He was watching her reaction as he said this, a seductive smile on his handsome face.

'I haven't time for a siesta,' Claire said quickly.

He laughed. 'I knew you would say that. You're very predictable . . . but come inside.'

He ushered her into a large entrance hall, which seemed to be filled with exotic tropical plants. They took the lift to the third floor, where a manservant opened the door to André's apartment. He hovered discreetly in the background until André, having poured two large glasses of cognac, dismissed him.

Claire felt a slight feeling of panic as the manservant disappeared. She sipped her cognac and glanced timidly round at the magnificent furnishings. The crimson and gold damask of the curtains was exactly matched in the antique chairs and sofa, the Chinese carpet blended in exquisitely, with just a subtle hint of Oriental charm. As André had said, it was a haven of peace.

'And what do you think of the cognac?' He was standing by the window, the afternoon sun shining on his hair.

She took another sip. 'It's . . . er . . . pleasant.'

'Pleasant!' He exploded with laughter.

'What did I say?' asked Claire innocently.

'I give you the most expensive cognac in France and you say it's pleasant. Oh Claire, you're adorable.'

He had crossed the room and sunk down beside her on the sofa. Gently he removed the glass from her hand and place it on a small antique table.

'I don't think you really like the cognac do you?' he smiled.

'It's . . . er . . . it's very strong.'

'It's too strong for you, I think,' he said. 'I'm trying to teach you too much, too quickly aren't I?' He cupped her face in his hands and stared into her wide blue eyes.

She held her breath as his lips came gently down on to hers. A shiver of delight went through her as his arms moved to caress her in a gentle embrace. With a sudden urgency he tightened his grip and lifted her off the sofa, carrying her effortlessly across the room and through a doorway.

'No, André,' she murmured feebly, but even as she spoke she knew she was lost. She felt powerless to quell the sensations arising inside her as the strong arms laid her gently on the soft quilt. His skilful, sensitive hands unbuttoned her silk jacket, and she shivered with ecstasy as he kissed her breasts. His hard body moved over hers and she closed her eyes in complete abandon. The movement of his delicate hands on her body was driving her frantic with an insatiable desire.

Suddenly he stopped and she opened her eyes to see him pulling himself away from her.

'No Claire. I can't take you like this.' His voice was breathless and tormented as he sat up and got off the bed. 'I shouldn't have brought you here.'

Claire pulled the silk jacket round her, trying desperately to return to reality. She lay on the bed panting breathlessly as she tried to regain her composure. Looking up at the ornate ceiling above her, she wondered how many seductions it had witnessed on this very bed. Her feelings of love turned to anger.

'I suppose this is where you bring all your girlfriends,' she said bitterly. 'Did you bring her here?'

'Who?' he asked, in a cold voice.

'Oh do stop pretending.' She stood up and moved quickly towards the door but André dashed in front of her, spreading his arms so that she could not escape.

'Don't go like this,' he said softly. 'There's something I must explain to you.'

'I don't want to hear it,' she said icily. 'I was a

fool to come here. Please let me pass.'

His arms dropped to his sides, in a gesture of resignation, and he stood back as she walked through the door.

'Pascal will let you out,' he said quietly, pressing a bell at the side of the door.

The manservant was standing by the main door when she arrived. He smiled at her deferentially as he opened the door.

'Would you like me to call a taxi for you madame?' he said.

'No thank you, Pascal,' she said evenly. 'I can manage.'

'*Au revoir*, madame,' he said politely.

'*Au revoir*,' said Claire and breathed a sigh of relief as the door closed behind her.

She stepped into the lift as if in a dream. Some of her composure had returned, but it wasn't until she was back in the Flament apartment that she began to feel truly alive again.

Simone came bounding towards her as she stepped out of the lift at the penthouse suite, and flung her little arms around her. 'I'm so glad you came back,' she shouted happily. 'The donkeys! We're going to see the donkeys!'

Claire smiled. She was back in the real world again. Her fantasy world had never really existed. She scooped the little girl up in her arms. 'First I've got to change out of this wretched suit, and then we'll go,' she said, going towards her room.

Marie had appeared in the corridor to see what all the noise was about. She smiled at Claire. 'Why do you call it a wretched suit, mademoiselle? It's beautiful,' she said appraisingly.

'No it's not. I hate it,' said Claire vehemently. 'I shall never wear it again. I'm going to throw it away.'

Marie's eyes widened. 'Don't throw it away mademoiselle. Give it to me. I would like it.'

'Would you, Marie? Would you really?'

The maid nodded.

'OK. I'll have it cleaned,' Claire said quickly.

'No, no mademoiselle. Give it to me. I'll take it to the cleaners. Here, put it in this bag.' The maid rushed into her room and came out with a large plastic bag.

Claire put Simone down. 'Wait here with Marie. I'll be back in a moment,' she said, hurrying to her room. Peeling off the hateful suit she stuffed it into the bag. Then, having slipped on the cotton dress she had worn that morning, she went back to Marie and Simone.

'Here you are, Marie,' she said, handing over the bag.

'Oh, thank you, mademoiselle,' said Marie gratefully. 'I shall wear it next month, I'm going to a wedding.'

Claire smiled. 'Yes, it will be most suitable,' she said wryly. 'Come on Simone, let's go to those donkeys.'

When they arrived at the Ranelagh Gardens, the donkey attendant greeted them like long-lost friends.

'*Enfin, vous arrivez*! I thought you were never coming. Here is your donkey waiting for you,' he called out excitedly, lifting Simone up on to its back.

'Hold on tight,' said Claire anxiously.

'Oh she will be quite safe, mademoiselle,' said the attendant. 'I will take care of her.'

The donkey had started to move forward, and Simone was squealing with delight. The attendant walked at the side, holding the donkey's reins, while Simone held on to the saddle. When the donkey ride was over, Simone pleaded to be allowed to stay on for another one. Claire, who was beginning to feel decidedly tired, felt in no mood to argue.

'Well, just one more, and then we'll go over to the sand-pit again,' she said.

Simone trotted off gleefully for another ride, after which she was reluctantly lifted down from the donkey's back.

They spent the rest of the afternoon in the sand pit, before making the short walk back to the apartment. As they stepped out of the lift, Claire noticed several expensive leather suitcases standing in the corridor.

'*Maman* is back!' said Simone excitedly. '*Maman*!' she called, running off down the corridor and bursting into her mother's room. '*Maman!*'

As Claire followed the little girl, she heard Hélène's voice saying crossly, 'I do think you might knock before you come in, Simone.'

Claire hovered in the open door. Hélène was stretched out on the bed.

'Ah there you are Nurse Baxter. Do you think you could take Simone away? I'm absolutely exhausted. I've had a terrible journey.'

'Why, certainly madame. I'm sorry you were disturbed. Come here Simone, *Maman* is very tired.'

Simone went over to Claire, and put her little hand in hers as Claire closed the door.

'*Maman* is having a rest. She's travelled a long way today, you know,' she said gently.

'Yes but I only wanted to see her,' said Simone, on the verge of tears. 'I haven't seen her for such a long time.'

'I know, you can see her later. Come along, we'll go to the nursery.'

Claire found herself remembering the words of Madame Thiret, 'Hélène is not the most ideal mother.' What an understatement. Perhaps it would be a good idea to take the children back to Arcachon, while she prepared Philippe for his operation. The relative peace and the sea air would do him good, and life was certainly much less complicated down there.

She went into the nursery suite and Marie immediately took charge.

'Mademoiselle, you do look tired,' she said.

'You've been dashing around all day. Let me look after Simone now.'

'Thank you, Marie. You'll call me if you need me?'

'Of course, mademoiselle. Madame Flament is back, but she said she didn't wish to be disturbed.'

'I know, Simone just went in to see her.'

'Oh dear,' the maid said. 'Was she cross?'

'Not exactly delighted,' laughed Claire.

'I should have warned you. Never mind. Go off and have a rest, mademoiselle.'

'Thanks, Marie. I'll see you later.' Claire went off to her room. She had a long relaxing bath and then lay down on the bed. Closing her eyes she fell asleep almost immediately.

Some time later there was a knock at the door. Claire awoke with a start and sat up, as Marie entered with a tray.

'I've brought you some supper. Madame Flament is having hers in her room, so I thought you might like some too.' The maid placed the tray on the bedside table.

'You are a dear,' said Claire. 'How's Simone?'

'Fast asleep, so no need to worry. I'll take care of her.'

'Thank you, Marie.'

The maid smiled and hurried away back to the nursery. Claire didn't feel the least bit hungry. I had too much lunch, she thought as she picked at the cold chicken and salad.

Her mind wandered back to the chic little restaurant, the intimate atmosphere, the handsome figure across the table . . . Tears sprang to her eyes but she dabbed at them mercilessly with a handkerchief, refusing to let them fall.

CHAPTER EIGHT

PHILIPPE arrived back from hospital the next day. André arrived mid-morning with him, carrying him gently in his arms, and brought him triumphantly into the nursery suite where Claire was giving Simone a short English lesson. The little girl jumped for joy when she saw her brother.

'Philippe!' she cried, running to him and reaching up her small arms.

André put Philippe down on a chair and Simone gave him a big kiss.

'Is he better now?' she asked her uncle.

'Not exactly,' he smiled at the little girl. 'He'll have to go back to hospital again in a few months, so we've all got to take great care of him.'

'I'll look after you, Philippe,' said Simone sweetly, stroking her brother's hand. 'You are my best brother,' she added in slow, but perfect English. Claire and André both laughed and looked at each other for the first time that day. As their eyes met, Claire looked away in embarrassment.

'Are you going to give me a full medical report?' she said briskly, in her most professional manner.

'Yes, of course,' he said, then glancing at the children, he asked, 'Where's Marie?'

'She's somewhere about. I'll get her to come and look after the children. Marie!' Claire went into the small nursery kitchen in search of the maid, glad of an excuse to cover her confusion.

When Marie was settled in the playroom with the children, André suggested they went to the drawing-room so they could talk.

They walked off down the corridor, Claire making sure there was a wide gap between them.

'I hear my sister has returned,' André said politely.

'Yes, but I've only seen her briefly. I think she's suffering from jet-lag.'

'Not surprising, it's a tiring journey,' he said.

They were like two strangers; there was no hint of the torrid relationship which had briefly existed yesterday.

André pushed open the drawing-room door and they went in to find Hélène sitting by the window. She was wearing a loose, flowing, ivory silk housecoat, and had obviously just got out of bed.

'Oh, André, I didn't know you were coming.' She pushed a hand through her unusually dishevelled hair. 'Forgive me, I'm not dressed yet.'

'You must be very tired,' André kissed his sister lightly on both cheeks. 'I've brought Philippe back.'

'Back? Where's he been?' she asked.

'He's been in hospital,' André said patiently.

'Why?' She sounded quite unconcerned.

'We've been giving him cardiac tests to determine the best course of action,' André started to explain. 'You see the essential function of the heart is to maintain an efficient circulation of blood. In Philippe's case . . .'

'Oh, for heaven's sake André,' Hélène interrupted, with a tinkling laugh. 'I can't possibly follow all your medical mumbo-jumbo. Tell Nurse Baxter about it. It doesn't interest me.'

Claire stared at her in disbelief.

'Oh, would you like some coffee, by the way?' Hélène went on, in the same uninterested voice.

'Yes, thank you,' André replied in a polite, but distant voice. 'Nurse Baxter, if you would like to sit here with me.'

They sat down on the sofa, and Hélène continued to gaze absently out of the window.

'Basically, we have decided to operate in three months' time,' he said, as if nothing had happened. 'There is some auricular fibrillation which is indicative of degeneration of the mitral valve, so we intend to do a replacement operation. In the meantime, I want you to give him good, general nursing care. There's no need to wrap him in cotton wool, but avoid exposing him to infection and don't allow him to over-exert himself. I would like him to be much stronger than he is now before we operate, but obviously if you note any increase in cardiac malfunctioning you must let me know at once.'

Claire nodded. 'I understand.'

'Well I'm glad you do,' said a bored voice from the window. 'How would you like your coffee?'

'Black.' They both spoke at once, and the resulting laughter helped to ease the tension.

'Come and join me here,' said Hélène petulantly. 'And stop all that medical talk. You both fuss too much.'

André raised his eyebrows in despair as they went over to sit by the window. He took the coffee cup his sister handed him.

'Wouldn't you like to see Philippe?' he asked.

'All in good time. I'm still very tired. I'll go along to the nursery when I'm dressed.'

'I've got tickets for the theatre tonight,' said André. 'Would you like to go Hélène? It's *Marie Tudor* at the Comédie Française.'

'*Marie Tudor*? Isn't that by Victor Hugo—heavens no! Much too serious for me. Why don't you take Nurse Baxter?'

Claire felt herself blushing furiously. 'Oh no, I couldn't possibly leave Philippe on his first night back,' she said, desperately trying to cover her emotion.

'Nonsense, Marie's perfectly capable—and anyway, I shall be here tonight.'

'Well that's a comfort,' said André in a sarcastic voice, which was lost on his sister. He turned to look at Claire. 'Would you like to go to the theatre Nurse Baxter? It's an essential part of your education, you know,' he added with only a hint of levity in his voice.

'Of course she'd like to go,' said Hélène. 'Have you ever been to the Comédie Française—no?—oh you must go there while you're here in Paris. André will take you tonight. That's settled.'

Without having said a word, Claire found that she was committed.

'I'll pick you up about eight-thirty,' André was saying.

'Why don't you dine with us first?' Hélène asked her brother.

'I haven't time tonight, Hélène. I have a very full schedule,' he said evenly.

'Well, don't be late André,' his sister said.

He stood up and embraced Hélène, nodding politely towards Claire. 'I have to go now. I'll see you this evening Nurse Baxter.'

As the door closed behind him, Claire turned to Hélène and said, 'Are you sure you don't want to go to the theatre, madame? I would really prefer to stay here with Philippe.'

'Don't be silly, you'll enjoy it. The Comédie Française is the most famous theatre in Paris. It will be a marvellous experience for you.'

'But . . . I've got nothing to wear,' she said desperately.

Hélène burst out laughing. 'Oh, my poor little Cinderella. Nothing to wear! That's no excuse. I've got plenty of clothes I can lend you—come along to my room. We'll see what we can find.' Hélène had jumped to her feet and was making for the door.

'Oh, no, madame. I couldn't possibly . . .' Claire began but Hélène cut her short.

'Of course you could. I'd be delighted to dress you. It is my job, after all. You're about my size—

perhaps a little slimmer, but I've got masses of stuff that will fit you.'

As she said this, Hélène was tripping lightly along the corridor and Claire decided she'd better follow. Hélène flung open her bedroom door and went over to her dressing-room. Claire gasped in amazement as she saw row after row of exquisite garments hanging from the rails. It resembled an expensive boutique or a fashion salon.

'Now let me see, here are some of my theatre-going outfits—oh, this would do perfectly! I designed it myself but I've never worn it,' Hélène said in an excited voice. 'With your colouring, it should be perfect.'

Claire looked at the stunning creation which Hélène was handing to her. It was a black, all-over pin-tucked cotton outfit, the dramatic jacket had a cleverly worked fluted frill, which echoed the swirling side-draped skirt. It was so beautiful it took her breath away.

'Well go on, try it!' said Hélène impatiently. 'I'm dying to see what it looks like on a good young figure.'

Claire slipped off her cotton dress and put on the outfit. Hélène clapped her hands in delight.

'It's a perfect fit, my dear. It might have been made for you. Looks a lot better on you than on me. You must keep it.'

Claire opened her mouth to remonstrate but Hélène silenced her. 'Now, no ifs or buts, child.' She laughed shortly. 'I'll never be able to wear it, now I've seen it on you. You look gorgeous! Come and look in the mirror.' She led Claire over to a full length mirror to admire the transformation.

'Now—shoes . . .' Hélène said. They both glanced at Claire's sensible brown walking sandals and laughed.

'They don't quite go with the outfit,' smiled Hélène. 'Let's see if I've got anything to fit you. Try these—oh, miles too big. You really are a Cinderella, aren't you?'

'I've got some black high-heeled strappy sandals that might do,' said Claire.

Hélène looked doubtful. 'Go and fetch them and we'll see.'

Claire hurried off to her room, barefoot but still in the stunning outfit. She danced a couple of twirls of delight, round the room, hardly recognising herself in the mirror as she did so. The black sandals were still wrapped in their original paper. They were an expensive pair, but she had bought them for a song at an end-of-season sale in London. She hastily put them on and went back to the dressing-room.

Hélène was delighted when she saw the shoes. 'Quite perfect, my dear. How clever of you,' she said. 'And now Cinderella may go to the ball,' she added in English, and they both laughed.

'Thank you so much, madame,' said Claire. 'I'm really looking forward to going out now. Clothes make such a difference.'

'Of course they do,' said Hélène.

'And when one is also accompanied by a very handsome gentleman, that too is a great pleasure, don't you think?' Her eyes were twinkling as she looked at Claire.

Claire found herself blushing, in spite of all her efforts not to. Hélène smiled at her.

'Don't you think my brother is attractive?' she asked coyly.

'There is no doubt he's very handsome,' said Claire evenly, without a trace of emotion.

'Yes, all the girls think so,' said Hélène.

Claire was silent.

'I must be getting back to the nursery now,' she said, after a few seconds.

'Yes, of course my dear. Oh, would you bring the children along to see me in about half an hour, when I've had my bath?'

'Certainly.' Claire gathered up her clothes and went to her room, where she changed back into her cotton dress.

The children greeted her happily when she arrived back in the nursery.

'Did you see *maman* this morning?' asked Philippe.

Claire scooped the little boy into her arms as she replied, 'Yes, and she wants to see you both in about half an hour.'

'That's nice,' said Philippe.

'Will you teach me some more English?' said Simone. 'And Philippe wants to learn too, don't you Philippe?'

Philippe nodded unenthusiastically. Claire sat him on her lap, with Simone at the side of her, and started going over the basic phrases they had been learning. Simone was quick to retain all the new vocabulary, but Philippe soon tired and was content to listen to his sister. When Claire felt that Hélène would be ready to receive them, she took the children along to her room.

'May I knock on the door?' asked Simone.

'Yes, you may—but gently please,' said Claire, remembering yesterday.

Simone knocked very quietly, so quietly that Hélène could not possibly have heard. They waited a few seconds, then Claire said cautiously, 'Just a little louder Simone.'

Before she could stop her, the little girl had banged loudly on the door several times.

'Oh, for goodness' sake,' came the irritable voice from inside. 'I suppose that's Simone again. Come in!'

They went in to find Hélène sitting at her desk, pencil in hand she was utterly absorbed in the sketches spread out in front of her. She turned as they went in and put out her hands to prevent Simone from jumping on her lap.

'Oh do be careful, Simone. These are very important designs, I don't want them all over the floor. Come over here where I can have a look at you both.' Hélène rose and went over to the *chaise-longue* by the window.

Claire put Philippe down beside Hélène, the

exuberant Simone had already climbed on her mother's lap.

'Mm, he looks a bit peaky, doesn't he?' Hélène turned to Claire. 'Needs some fresh air I'd say, what do you think Nurse?'

'Yes, he is rather pale,' said Claire. 'But then it's all part of his condition.'

'Condition? Oh, stuff and nonsense! You're beginning to sound more and more like André. All children need lots of fresh air—I know that much. Take them out for a walk. It'll do them good.'

She removed Simone from her lap and stood up. 'I'll see you all later. *Au revoir mes enfants*,' she said, returning to her desk.

'*Au revoir, Maman*,' they dutifully replied, as they trotted out of the door.

'Well, that was a short visit!' said Marie, when they returned to the nursery.

Claire laughed. 'Madame Flament is not over-endowed with maternal instinct,' she whispered to Marie. 'Two minutes with her offspring and she's had enough. I'm going to take them out for a walk.'

'Would you like me to come with you, mademoiselle?' said Marie, helpfully. 'I can keep an eye on Simone while you're looking after Philippe.'

'Yes that would be a great help,' said Claire. 'But won't you be needed here?'

'No I've finished my nursery duties. I shan't be needed until lunchtime now. Shall we see if Henri can take us over to the Bois de Boulogne? It's lovely by the lake.'

'Oh yes.' Simone had been listening to the last part of the conversation and was jumping up and down in anticipation. 'Let's go to see the ducks. I'll get some bread.' She dashed off into the little kitchen, and came back carrying a *demi-baguette* left over from breakfast.

Claire smiled at Marie. 'It seems like we're going to the Bois de Boulogne,' she said wryly.

'I'll ring down to Henri,' said Marie, picking up the internal phone.

Claire took the children to their rooms to prepare them for the outing, then, loaded with a variety of bags, they all went down in the lift to the underground car-park.

Henri was waiting for them and put their things in the boot. Marie sat in front with Henri, and Claire sat on the back seat with Philippe on her lap, and Simone by her side. The car purred gently down the Boulevard towards the Bois de Boulogne, coming to a halt when they reached the lake. Henri got out to help Marie and Claire with the children.

'Shall I come with you, mesdemoiselles?' he asked.

'No, thank you, Henri. We shall be all right,' said Claire. 'Will you wait here for us?'

Certainly, mademoiselle.' The good-natured chauffeur climbed back into the car, pulling a packet of Gauloise from his pocket.

They negotiated the path down to the lake and found a convenient seat right by the side of it.

Philippe sat on Claire's lap, but Simone crouched by the water's edge throwing chunks of bread out for the ducks.

'Don't go too near, or you'll fall in,' said Claire.

'I think I'd better hold her hand,' said Marie, going over to the little girl.

The ducks swam across the sunlit water, quacking noisily when they saw the bread being thrown in the water. Philippe gave a gentle smile as he watched them, but made no move to leave Claire. Soon the ducks were joined by two swans, so Claire decided it was time to move on.

'Come on, Marie, we'd better go a little further away. Swans can sometimes be dangerous,' she called, looking at the powerful birds as they glided towards them through the water.

Marie took charge of Simone, still clutching her bread, and Claire gathered little Philippe into her arms. Together they walked along the path by the lakeside, until they were opposite the island where André had taken Claire on that first day, which now seemed so long ago. She looked across at the island, trying to remember what André had been like before she began to know him.

Marie spread a rug on the grass, and Claire showed the children how to make daisy chains. While Simone was happy to pick the daisies, Philippe enjoyed sitting on the rug, threading the flowers into the stems.

'This is a necklace for *Maman*,' he said proudly, as he held up the intricate work which had taken him such a long time to make.

'It's beautiful,' said Claire.

'Do you think she'll like it?' the little boy asked anxiously.

'I'm sure she will,' said Claire hopefully. 'Now, I think we'd better be making a move—mustn't be late for lunch.'

Claire and Marie gathered up the things and they all started to walk back towards the car. As they climbed the steep path to the road, Henri came running to meet them.

'Let me help you,' he said, taking the bags from Claire and Marie. They reached the roadside and climbed into the car. Philippe sat on Claire's lap clutching the precious daisy necklace in his tiny fingers. Henri drove them back and parked in the underground car-park.

Soon they were speeding upwards towards the penthouse suite. As the doors opened they all spilled out into the corridor in a noisy rush. Hélène's door opened and she came out furiously.

'Is there no peace in this house?' she said icily. 'I'm trying to work in here.'

'I'm sorry madame,' said Claire quietly. 'The children are a little excited.'

'Well I do wish you would keep them quiet. I can't bear noise when I'm working.' She started to go back into her room.

'*Maman*,' Philippe's little voice rang out down the corridor. 'I've made you a necklace.'

The little boy took a few hesitant steps towards

his mother. She turned and looked at the wilting flowers he was holding out.

'That's very sweet of you,' she said absently. 'Ask Marie to put them in water.'

'But it's a necklace, *Maman*,' he said falteringly, but his mother's door was already closed. He looked round helplessly and Claire quickly scooped him up into her arms, before his tears could fall.

'I'll look after it for you, until Mummy wants to wear it,' she said, taking the daisy chain from his hands, but the little boy had already lost interest. 'I think we'll have lunch in the nursery,' said Claire to Marie. 'Madame is obviously in a working mood.'

'That's a good idea,' said Marie. 'Let's see if cook is ready for us.'

Marie went along to the kitchen and Claire took the children to their rooms to wash their hands. Marie served lunch in the tiny nursery dining-room for the four of them. It was a pleasant relaxed meal, no fuss, no frills and they all enjoyed it—even Philippe, who seemed to have forgotten his disappointment at his mother's reaction to his present. Cook had made delicious lamb chops with *petits pois* and this was followed by a fruit salad.

Afterwards Claire carried the sleepy Philippe to his bed, while Simone tiptoed to her own room and lay down for her rest. Both children were soon fast asleep, so Claire took a book out on to the roof garden and sat down among the tropical plants. The afternoon sun was very hot, so she stayed partly in the shade. Very soon the book slipped from her hands and she too, fell asleep.

She was awakened some time later by the sound of Hélene shouting down the corridor.

'What's the use of having people to look after the children if I have to do everything myself.'

Claire jumped up hastily and ran across the roof garden.

'Ah there you are Nurse,' said Hélène, coolly. 'I do wish you would keep Simone out of my room when I'm working. I have to have these designs finished by the end of the week.'

Simone, looking utterly crestfallen, was standing by her mother.

'I waked up, and couldn't find you,' she said, trotting towards Claire. 'Can we go and feed the ducks?'

'No, we fed the ducks this morning, but we'll find something to do. Come back to the nursery, Simone,' she said briskly, taking hold of Simone's hand and adding, 'I'm sorry you were disturbed, madame. It won't happen again.'

'I should hope not,' said Hélène crossly, slamming the door as she returned to her room.

That's it! thought Claire. We simply must go back to Arcachon. Madame Thiret will welcome us with open arms, and Hélène will be able to have all the peace and quiet she requires. I'll see what André thinks tonight.

She found Marie sitting in Philippe's room when she got back to the nursery. When the children were out of earshot, she told her of the latest episode with Hélène.

'That woman!' stormed Marie. 'She just lives for her work. I don't know why she ever had children.'

'Oh, she's had her problems, I suppose,' said Claire, in a soothing voice. 'But I'm going to suggest we go back to Arcachon for the rest of the summer. It will be much better for the children there.'

'Oh, I shall miss you,' said Marie sadly. 'And the children. I wonder . . .' she looked thoughtful. 'I wonder if I could come down with you. I mean, there's nothing for me to do here, when the children are away, and I'm sure I could help you with them.'

'You most certainly could,' said Claire enthusiastically. 'I think it's a brilliant idea. I'll put it to Madame Flament this evening.' It would be such a help having Marie to cope with Simone's high spirits, while she devoted her attention to Philippe.

They amused the children in the nursery until supper-time, when Marie told Claire she would look after the children while she prepared herself for the theatre.

'But you must come and show us your beautiful gown, before you go,' said Marie.

'Of course I will.' Claire smiled happily, as she thought of the beautiful outfit. Her heart fluttered in wild anticipation of the evening ahead. She went to her room, and soaked herself gently in soothing bath foam. She patted herself dry with one of the fluffy towels and sprinkled herself liberally with expensive eau de toilette. Then, carefully pulling on the dramatic outfit, she faced herself in the mirror.

What a startling transformation!

The only thing that was wrong was her long blonde hair. It was not sophisticated enough. She sat down and started to brush it vigorously. A pair of scissors was sitting on her dressing-table. She eyed them thoughtfully . . . no—better not, she decided. She remembered the silver Spanish comb her grandmother had worn in her hair. Claire always carried it everywhere she went, as a memento, but she'd never yet dared to wear it. Rummaging through her trinkets box, she found it. Now, if only she had a few hairpins . . .

There was a gentle tap on the door and Marie hovered on the threshold.

'Marie!' she cried. 'Just the girl I'm looking for. Have you got any hairpins?'

'Mademoiselle, you look beautiful! I came to say the children are in bed and they want to see you. Hairpins, you say? Wait here—I'll fetch some.'

She was back in a few seconds, carrying a box of hairpins which she set down on the dressing-table.

'Let me fix your hair for you. I used to do this for my sisters,' she said confidently. 'They're all married now, so it worked! Keep stil, mademoiselle.' The deft fingers were twining the hair up on top of Claire's head, expertly pinning it in position. The silver comb, set at the back of the head, added the final touch.

'There,' said Maire, obviously pleased with her handiwork. 'How's that?'

Claire stared at the sophisticated lady in the mirror. Was this really her? She stood up and twirled round with delight.

'Thank you, Marie. You're wonderful!'

'Don't forget to ask madame if I can come with you to Arcachon,' said the maid, smiling happily.

'I most certainly will not. Let's go and see the children now, before they fall asleep.'

Simone's eyes widened when she saw Claire. 'You look like a princess,' she said truthfully.

'Thank you,' said Claire, giving the little girl a hug.

Philippe was almost asleep but he smiled at Claire and put out a little hand to touch her dress.

'Pretty,' he said softly, as he closed his eyes.

Claire kissed him gently on the forehead and tiptoed quietly out.

Hélène was waiting for her when she arrived in the drawing-room. 'You look quite splendid, my dear,' she said appraisingly. 'If you ever want to give up nursing, I can find you a job as a mannequin. Would you like a drink before dinner?'

'Yes please.'

'Kir?'

Claire nodded. 'Lovely.'

They sat by the window to drink their aperitifs.

'I'm sorry I was so . . . er . . . impatient with the

children today,' said Hélène. 'I can't help it. They really do irritate me when I'm working. It's not their fault—they just get in the way.'

Claire was silent for a few seconds before she said, 'Do you think it would be a good idea if I took the children back to Arcachon for a while? The sea air would be so good for Philippe and you would find it easier to work here without them.'

Hélène brightened visibly. 'I think you're right, my dear. Yes, the sea air would be excellent for the children. I can't get away just now, otherwise I'd join you.'

'Oh don't worry,' Claire said hastily. 'Perhaps Marie could come with me?'

'That's an excellent idea. I'll ring Madame Thiret tonight. I expect she'll be delighted.'

'I'm sure she will,' said Claire.

They went into dinner, Claire feeling slightly conspicuous in her superb outfit. By the side of her plate there was a small packet, with the name of one of the most chic boutiques in Paris.

'What's this?' said Claire in surprise, as she sat down.

'Oh that's the bag I bought to go with that outfit,' said Hélène casually. 'I thought you might like it.'

Claire opened the packet and found a small black leather evening bag.

'You must have guessed I didn't have one,' she said to Hélène.

'Oh, haven't you got one?' asked Hélène nonchalantly. 'Well I simply thought it would complement the outfit.'

'Thank you very much,' Claire said with real feeling.

'You're most welcome.' Hélène smiled a dazzling smile. 'It makes me very happy to see one of my designs looking so good. There's one thing—you won't see another one like it in Paris.'

They both laughed. The maid served the first course, which was *sole meunière*. This was followed by a game dish called *pintade*, which was guinea fowl cooked in a wine and mushroom sauce. As she finished the delicious guinea fowl, Claire glanced at her watch and was surprised to see it was almost eight-thirty.

'Will you excuse me, madame? It's almost time for Dr Dubois to arrive and I have some things to collect from my room.'

'Why of course, my dear. Run along. My brother hates to be kept waiting.'

'I know.' Claire smiled at Hélène as she picked up the new bag and left the table.

Back in her room she carefully put a liptstick, a hankerchief and a few francs into the bag before returning to the dining-room.

'André still hasn't arrived,' said Hélène petulantly. 'I wonder what can be keeping him. You'll have to go soon or you'll be late.'

At that moment, the door opened and André burst in.

'I've got a taxi waiting downstairs. Are you ready?' he said uncermoniously.

'You're late, André,' said Hélène in a scolding voice. 'Nurse Baxter has been ready for ages.'

'I couldn't help it,' he said breathlessly. 'We had an emergency. I was in the operating theatre until half an hour ago.' He looked tense and tired, but his expression changed as Claire came towards him.

'Wow!' he whistled softly and uncharacteristically. 'You look . . .' he seemed to be searching for the right words, '*tout à fait magnifique!*'

'Yes, doesn't she,' Hélène agreed, while Claire tried to look cool and poised.

'Have a nice time,' said Hélène, as André took Claire's arm and steered her through the doorway.

They went down to the waiting taxi, which hurtled across Paris at an incredible speed, screeching to a halt in front of the Comédie Française. They went up the steps of the ancient, ornate stone building and into a cool, high-ceilinged foyer. An usherette came forward.

'The play is about to start, monsieur. Come this way quickly.' She led the way into the theatre, where the lights had already been dimmed. It was smaller than Claire had expected, for which she was grateful, as their seats were very near the front. She hurried along behind André, trying not to stumble in the semi-darkness. The curtains rose as they took their places, but the first scene was so dark that Claire still could not see very much of the interior of the theatre. She had an impression of comfortable plush seats and a crowded house, but that was all. She tried desperately to get the gist of the play but found it rather boring and incomprehensible. It was with relief that she saw the curtain fall at the end of the first act.

'Let's go to the bar,' said André, as soon as the lights went up. 'I could do with a drink—how about you?'

'Yes, that would be lovely,' she said, trying to stand up without spoiling her skirt. '*Excusez-moi,*' she said to the man in the next seat, as she attempted to push her way through to the aisle as elegantly as possible. André was right behind her, he had put his hand on her waist, presumably to help her along, but it was doing nothing for her composure. The faint perfume of his after-shave was beginning to make her nervous.

They reached the bar, and André ordered champagne.

What else! thought Claire. This man is impossible.

She was aware that heads were turning as she passed. It was a delicious feeling—one to which she could easily become accustomed, she decided. André's eyes showed his obvious admiration as they sat down at a corner table.

'Are you enjoying the play?' he asked.

'Well it's a little difficult to understand,' she said truthfully.

'Yes, I agree. The first act is a difficult one.

You'll enjoy the later scenes—there's much more action.'

He's still playing his dutiful part of cultural teacher, thought Claire. It makes things easier this way.

She put her hand over her champagne glass as André was about to replenish it.

'Don't worry,' he smiled. 'I'll take you straight home tonight, I promise. My intentions are truly honourable,' he added wryly. 'Do have some more champagne, as I told you, it doesn't keep.'

Claire relented and allowed her glass to be topped up. It will make the play more bearable, she thought.

Whether it was the effects of the champagne, or an improvement in the play, Claire found the concluding scenes to be much more enjoyable. The final act, especially, was full of life, and excitement, and she found herself clapping wildly at the end as the cast returned for several curtain-calls. As the actors left the stage for the final time, and the applause died down, Claire turned to see that André was watching her with a strange expression on his face.

'Let's go,' he said brusquely.

'Why, of course,' Claire said, making her way to the central aisle. They went out through the foyer into the moonlit Parisian night. André found a taxi and they were soon speeding along the side of the Seine. The lights from the river boats twinkled merrily in the darkness, and Claire remembered, with a pang, that she would soon be leaving Paris.

'André, do you mind if I take Philippe to Arcachon?' she said. 'I think it will be easier to look after the children down there. After all, Hélène has her work . . .'

André laughed. 'You're right—Hélène has her work, and hates to be disturbed. It's a good idea. I'll come down whenever I can. It's time I went back to Arcachon,' he added softly.

Claire looked at the handsome face, outlined by the bright lights of Paris. If only she knew what he were thinking. I suppose this gives him a good excuse to go back to Arcachon and Pat Johnson . . .

He had turned to look at her. 'Yes, make all the necessary arrangements. I trust you implictly,' he said evenly.

'Thank you,' she said softly. There was a lump in her throat and she had the awful feeling that she was going to cry. She stared fixedly out of the window at the tumultuous traffic. André's hand closed suddenly over hers and he pulled her towards him.

'What about your boyfriend?' he asked roughly. 'Won't he miss you?'

'He may do,' said Claire truthfully. 'I don't really know.' She could feel her heart beating wildly as André held her near to him. As the taxi reached the Flament apartment she tried to move away but he was still holding her close. With one of his hands he gently removed the pins from her hair until the blonde tresses cascaded round her shoulders.

'There, that's better,' he said, running his fingers through her hair. 'That's the way I like to see you.' She felt his lips lightly kiss her hair and then, almost at once, he pulled open the taxi door and leapt out. He turned to help her out, but as she moved across the pavement, thinking he would follow her, he put a restraining hand on her arm.

'I'm not coming in tonight, Claire,' he said, with what seemed to be a great effort. He was breathing heavily as he faced her. 'I have to go back to the hospital to see my emergency patient. *Bonsoir*.' He bent down and kissed her lightly on the cheek.

'*Bonsoir*,' she said and hurried quickly up the front staircase. It was only as she reached the top step that she put a hand to her loose flowing hair, remembering the silver comb. She turned quickly but the taxi was already roaring off down the Boulevard.

She experienced a feeling of relief and disappointment, as the lift climbed up to the penthouse suite. She wondered if André had invented the emergency patient to prevent them being alone together. No matter, she reminded herself again, it was easier this way.

Marie was waiting up for her in the nursery kitchen.

'Oh, you've taken your hair down,' she smiled knowingly, and Claire blushed, trying to cover her confusion by asking about the children.

'They're both sleeping peacefully and their cases are packed for the morning,' Marie answered in reply to her question.

'For the morning?' echoed Claire, in surprise. 'That was quick.'

'Yes, Madame Flament came along here after dinner and asked me to pack, ready for an early start tomorrow. She told me to tell you that Madame Thiret is delighted.'

Claire smiled. 'I knew she would be. Well, Madame Flament hasn't wasted much time, has she?'

'Can't wait to get rid of us,' chuckled Marie. 'Oh, I almost forgot. There was a phone call for you—someone called Robert, said he'd ring back later. He's rung twice already, I hope Madame Flament has switched the phone off in her room, or she'll be furious—ah! There it goes again.'

Claire quickly picked up the phone. 'Robert, you shouldn't phone me so late . . .' she started but he broke in.

'I've been phoning you all evening. Where've you been?' he said crossly.

'I've been to the theatre,' she said evenly.

'With your doctor, I suppose,' he said furiously.

'He's not *my* doctor—and anyway it's no concern of yours,' she said icily.

'Yes it *is* my concern—I love you Claire.'

'Oh please . . . not now Robert, not over the phone,' she whispered.

'Then when? When can I see you?'

'I don't know, Robert. We're going back to Arcachon tomorrow.'

'Tomorrow—oh Claire. Don't go . . . please don't go.'

'Don't be silly, Robert. I have to go. It's my job. I'll give you a ring when I can.'

There was silence at the other end of the line.

'Robert?' said Claire after a few seconds.

'Goodbye, Claire,' he said coldly.

'Goodbye,' she said, putting down the phone with a flood of relief.

Marie smiled gently at her.

'The course of true love never runs smooth,' she said wisely.

'No, Marie.' Claire sighed wistfully as she crossed to the door of the little kitchen. '*Bonsoir*. I'll see you bright and early tomorrow.'

'*Bonsoir*, mademoiselle.'

CHAPTER NINE

AMID the bustle of activity next morning Claire had no time to think about the events of the previous evening. By nine o'clock they were driving south along the motorway, Henri having insisted they made an early start so that they could avoid the traffic in Paris.

It was mid-afternoon when they reached Arcachon. Madame Thiret came out on to the front steps to greet them, when she heard the car scrunching on the gravel drive.

'Welcome, my dear,' she said kindly to Claire. 'And Marie is here too—that's nice. An extra pair of hands is always useful. Come inside, I'll show you to your rooms.'

She led the way to Claire's bedroom, the same cool, cream-coloured room overlooking the sea, which Claire remembered so well. Then, with a slight twinkle in her eye, she opened the door of the room next to it.

'I've had the maids prepare this one for the children,' she said. 'It'll be more convenient for you. And I thought we could put Marie in the next room on the other side of the children.'

Claire smiled at the old lady. 'Thank you, madame,' she said softly.

'Well, now, if you'd like to unpack, I'll see you all

at supper-time,' said the old lady brusquely. 'Seven o'clock sharp—don't be late,' she added as she started off down the stairs.

They spent the rest of the afternoon settling into their rooms. Marie took Simone to the beach to work off some of the high spirits which had been suppressed throughout the car journey, and Claire was able to devote her attention to Philippe.

Supper was served promptly at seven and Madame Thiret nodded approvingly to find Claire and the children sitting at the table when she entered the room. She sat down at the head of the table as usual, and served home-made vegetable soup from the steaming blue and white porcelain tureen.

'I'm not hungry,' whispered Philippe to Claire, as a small bowl was place in front of him.

'You must eat a little,' she whispered back, picking up his spoon as she tried to coax him to taste the soup. He sighed and opened his mouth, allowing Claire to feed him a few spoonfuls, before he shook his head wearily.

'He's very tired tonight,' said Claire to Madame Thiret, who had been watching with an air of disapproval. 'I think I'll put him to bed.'

'Well, eat your supper first,' she said sternly to Claire. 'Philippe can sit over here on the sofa until you're ready for him.'

Philippe got down from the table with an air of relief and, climbing on to the sofa, he lay back among the cushions.

Madame Thiret leaned forward towards Claire and whispered, 'The sooner something is done about that boy the better.'

'Don't worry, madame,' said Claire. 'Dr Dubois has got everything under control.'

'Well, I certainly hope so,' said the old lady anxiously.

Claire was finishing her soup when the maid brought in the next course.

'Chicken,' said Madame Thiret. 'I ordered it specially, because it's good for delicate little tummies.' She glanced at Philippe, who was now asleep on the sofa. 'Ah well, Simone, you will have some won't you?'

'Yes, please, madame,' said Simone holding out her plate. She proceeded to eat everything that was placed in front of her, finishing off with a large ice-cream.

At the end of supper Marie came in to collect Simone, and Claire picked up the sleeping Philippe in her arms.

'*Bonsoir*, madame,' she said. 'I'm going to stay in my room. I'm feeling rather tired.'

The old lady nodded, smiling. '*Bonsoir*, mademoiselle. *Dormez bien*.'

Claire carried Philippe upstairs into the children's room. Marie was getting Simone ready for bed. She smiled at Claire when she went in.

'We'll have to be very quiet,' she whispered to Simone, 'We mustn't disturb Philippe.'

Claire laid the little boy down on his bed and

gently undressed him. He stirred slightly in his sleep, but didn't open his eyes. Claire pulled the covers over him and sat down on the bed to watch him. She felt his pulse anxiously. There was a slight irregularity which had not been there that morning. The journey has tired him, she thought. We must take it easy tomorrow. She bent down and kissed him gently on the forehead.

Marie had succeeded in settling Simone into her bed, although she still looked wide awake. Claire tiptoed across the room.

'You will be quiet, won't you Simone,' she whispered. 'Philippe is very tired.'

Simone smiled and nodded, stretching her little arms towards her. Claire bent down and gave her a kiss.

'*Bonsoir chérie.*'

'*Bonsoir.*' The little girl turned over and closed her eyes obediently.

Claire and Marie went out into the corridor and closed the door.

'I'm going to have an early night Marie,' said Claire. 'Thank you for your help. I'll see you in the morning.'

'Yes, *bonsoir*, mademoiselle.'

'*Bonsoir*, Marie.' Claire went into her room and closed the door. She went over to the window and looked out at the now familiar view. The sun was beginning to set on the horizon, casting a crimson glow on the water. A lone yacht was sailing back into the harbour, its sails alight with the fiery red of the evening rays. She thought of another yacht, where she had been so happy, before the arrival of that other woman—before she had heard those fateful words, 'André asked me to marry him.'

Briskly she turned from the window and went into the little bathroom. There was no point dwelling on it now.

When she awoke, the sun was already streaming in through the window.

Heavens, it must be very late, she thought, jumping out of bed with a rush. After a hasty shower, she flung her clothes on and went into the children's room. Marie was already there, and the children were washed and dressed.

'Oh Marie, you are a dear. I think I must have overslept,' she said.

'I didn't want to waken you, mademoiselle. I thought the sleep would do you good.'

'Thank you. Yes, I feel much better this morning.'

Claire sat down on Philippe's bed and put the little boy on her lap. Carefully she took his pulse, then checked and rechecked. Yes, the irregularity was still there. If only André was here. I'll ring him at lunchtime, she thought. He's probably at the hospital now. Meanwhile I'm not taking any chances. She gave him the medication which André had prescribed, then carried him down to breakfast. Madame Thiret did not comment on the fact that he sat on Claire's lap throughout the meal.

'Are we going to the Mickey Club?' asked

Simone brightly, as she got down from the table.

'Perhaps Marie would like to take you, would you Marie?' said Claire. 'I'm going to stay here with Philippe.'

'Yes, of course I'll take you,' said Marie, taking hold of Simone's hand.

'Henri will drive you there,' said Madame Thiret stiffly.

'Thank you madame,' said Marie, as she took the little girl upstairs.

'We're going to spend a quiet morning in the garden,' said Claire.

'Very wise,' said Madame Thiret. 'The sun is already very hot. Best to keep in the shade.'

Claire carried Philippe out into the garden and sat him on a rug beneath the trees. He remained still and listless while she went off to gather some daisies. When she brought them back he began to show a little interest, but his little fingers had difficulty in threading the flowers today.

'You make it,' he said softly to Claire, after an initial feeble attempt.

Claire made a little daisy chain and placed it round her neck. He smiled briefly.

'That's nice,' he said quietly. 'You look pretty.'

Claire smiled at the little boy and lifted him on to her lap. He was quite content to sit looking out to sea, watching the boats sailing past. When she looked closer, she saw he had fallen asleep.

Just before lunchtime the sound of car wheels on the gravel drive announced that Simone and Marie had arrived back from the Mickey Club. The little girl came running across the grass towards them.

'Philippe! Philippe!' she called excitedly. 'I had a lovely time. I ran in a race and I won a prize.'

Philippe awoke with a start and, climbing off Claire's lap, he began to walk towards his sister. He took several feeble steps before falling forward on to the grass.

'Philippe.' Claire was at his side immediately. One look at the pale, cyanosed face confirmed her fears.

'Marie,' she called. 'Take Simone into the house, and get Dr Dubois on the phone for me. And ask Henri to bring the emergency box from my room.'

'Yes, mademoiselle.' Marie had assessed the seriousness of the situation and was hurrying into the house, pulling Simone with her.

Claire bent over the prostrate little figure. His breathing had stopped. She pinched the tiny nostrils between her fingers, as she breathed gently into the lifeless mouth. After several seconds, which seemed like an eternity, there was a response. His lungs started to move again by themselves and the little blue eyes opened briefly.

'Oh, Philippe,' she murmured breathlessly. She picked up the rug and wrapped it round him as Henri arrived with the emergency box. With deft fingers, she extricated the oxygen mask and clamped it over the little boy's face.

'Nurse Baxter!' Madame Thiret's voice came

from the house. 'I have Dr Dubois on the phone for you.'

'Follow me,' said Claire briefly, handing the oxygen cylinder to the white-faced Henri, as she carried her precious bundle into the house. She sat down by the phone, still holding Philippe, while Madame Thiret held the instrument for her.

'André, thank God!' she said. 'Philippe has had a cardiac arrest. I've given him mouth-to-mouth resuscitation and he's breathing again, with the help of oxygen.'

'Take him straight to Bordeaux hospital—I'll ring them now,' said the reassuring voice. 'I'll be there in a couple of hours—my plane is on standby. Are you all right?'

'Yes, I'm all right,' she said, in a surprised voice. 'But hurry, I need you.'

'I need you too,' was the cryptic reply. 'Goodbye.'

The phone went dead.

Claire carried Philippe out to the car and told Henri what André had said. Grimly he let in the clutch and the car moved forward down the drive. As they pulled out into the road, Claire could see the distraught figure of Madame Thiret standing on the steps.

The car sped along the motorway towards Bordeaux. Claire regulated the flow of oxygen to her precious patient, he was breathing easily now and was a better colour. She took out her stethoscope and checked the apex-beat. There was still a marked discrepancy with the pulse-rate, indicating malfunction of the mitral valve. Philippe's eyes were closed and she found herself praying desperately for his survival.

As they reached the outskirts of Bordeaux the green vineyards flashed past in a blurred haze.

What if André is delayed? she thought. What shall I do without him? But she checked her thoughts. One step at a time . . . Philippe is still alive . . . let's take it from there.

Henri pulled up in front of the hospital, and opening the car door, he helped Claire and her patient inside. A nursing sister came to meet them.

'You must be Nurse Baxter,' she said reassuringly. 'Dr Dubois has phoned us with the case history. Nurse!' she called.

A nurse and a porter arrived simultaneously with a trolley.

'You may leave Philippe with us,' the sister said gently. 'We'll take him straight to intensive care until Dr Dubois arrives.'

'I'd like to go with him,' said Claire anxiously.

'As you wish,' smiled the sister. 'But he is in good hands. Why don't you take a break? We'll call you when Dr Dubois arrives.'

The sister removed Philippe from Claire's arms and placed him on the trolley, where he lay pale and inert, breathing into the oxygen mask. The nurse gently took hold of Claire's arm.

'If you would like to come with me, Nurse Baxter . . .'

Claire allowed herself to be led through a maze of corridors to a large staff common-room. It was only then that she realised how tense and tired she was. This was no ordinary patient. This was a child she loved with all her heart. How had she managed to become so involved? Was it because the child, in spite of his fragile frame, bore an uncanny resemblance to his maddeningly irresistible uncle? The nurse handed her a cup of strong black coffee.

'Here, take this . . . you look as if you need it.'

'Thanks,' said Claire, smiling briefly at the young nurse. She sank back into an armchair and closed her eyes. Please hurry, André, she whispered to herself. Please be on time. The minutes ticked by, he had said two hours. She glanced at her watch, the two hours were nearly up. The wall phone bleeped and the nurse answered it at once.

'It's for you,' she said, briefly.

Claire sprang to the phone, and was relieved to hear André's voice.

'Where are you?' she asked.

'I'm with Philippe in intensive care. We've decided to operate now—would you like to be there?'

'Oh yes,' Claire said with conviction.

'Well, keep out of the way,' he said ungraciously. 'I've got first class staff round the table, but I thought you might like to see what's going on.'

'Thank you, yes I would.' Suddenly her manner reverted to that of junior nurse confronted by senior surgeon. 'I'll see you in theatre.'

'Yes, goodbye,' he said and the line went dead.

'They're going to operate,' she said to the nurse. 'Would you show me the way to the theatre?'

'Certainly,' said the young nurse, as she sprang to open the door.

Claire went through and the nurse led her down the corridor, up a flight of stairs and through to the operating theatres.

The scrub-room was a hive of activity. Theatre Sister indicated a shower-cubicle which she could use, and she stripped off and soaped herself furiously under the hot water. As she emerged a nurse handed her a towel, and then helped her into a sterile gown and mask. The babble of voices died down as the great man himself came through the double doors and was carefully prepared by the willing minions who danced attention upon him. Claire caught a glimpse of the tense, dark eyes above the mask, but if he even noticed her he did not acknowledge the fact. The doors to the theatre were opened, and they went in. The anaesthetist was bending over a tiny prostrate figure on the table. Could this really be Philippe?

Claire hovered in the background, careful not to get in the way, but anxious to see as much as possible. She saw Theatre Sister hand a scalpel to André. He made the first incision and bent over the tiny form to start the delicate valve replacement operation.

She marvelled at his concentration as time passed. The theatre staff were tiring, but André looked as fresh as when he started, calling briefly for swabs, instruments and finally for the sutures with which to close the wound.

As he straightened up at the end of the operation, there was a visible relaxation of the tension inside the theatre. He turned to walk out of the theatre and there was a murmur of approval. Claire stood back to let the great man pass, and the dark eyes above the mask seemed to notice her for the first time. The swing doors closed and he was gone. Claire watched as Philippe was wheeled away, then threw herself into the task of helping the nurses clear the theatre. When she had finished, she went out and found her way into a shower cubicle. She found she was wet through with nervous perspiration, as she stripped off the sticky theatre gown and stepped under the shower. The water cascaded down, helping to soothe her weary body. The noise of the water made her deaf to all other sounds, so that she heard nothing until the shower curtain was wrenched aside.

Gasping furiously, she reached for a towel as André smiled at her through the dripping water. She flung her towel round her with one hand, turning off the water with the other.

'How dare you!' she spluttered.

'Oh, please—no false modesty—I came to find you, and I thought someone had left the shower on.' He grinned mischievously, and trailed his hand lightly across the top of her towel. Her legs started to melt beneath her. She looked into the dark, beguiling eyes.

'You're a wicked liar,' she murmured softly.

'I know,' he said, as his mouth closed over hers. His hands were gently feeling for her breasts as the towel fell to the floor. She pressed her naked body against the hard, masculine form in an overwhelming surge of irresistible passion. The world ceased to exist, as she lost herself in his embrace.

'Dr Dubois!' From somewhere beyond time, a harsh voice was calling her back to reality.

'André!' She pushed him away and fled into the shower cubicle as Theatre Sister arrived through the door.

'Ah, there you are, Dr Dubois,' she said. 'We're ready for you now in intensive care.'

'Thank you, Sister.' The professional voice of the surgeon held no trace of emotion as he followed the sister out.

Alone in the shower cubicle, Claire turned on the water again. This time she turned the cold tap, in an effort to dampen her overwhelming feeling of frustration.

She dabbed herself dry and put on her clothes. She was floating on cloud nine as she emerged from the theatre. She went down the corridor and suddenly her dream was shattered. Standing in front of the door to intensive care was a slim, elegant figure.

'I came as soon as I heard,' Pat Johnson said. 'How is he?'

Claire stared at her. 'I don't know yet,' she muttered. 'He came through the operation, and he's now in intensive care.'

'Oh, do you think I could see him?' asked Pat.

'Your concern is very touching,' said Claire icily. 'But I doubt if you'll be allowed to see him.' She was aware of a slight movement behind her and turned to see André towering above her.

'I wasn't aware that you made the rules here, Nurse,' he said in a cold professional voice.

Claire stared at him in disbelief.

He turned his attention to Pat. 'If you'd like to wait here,' he said politely, 'I'll ask Sister to let you in for a few minutes.' With that he disappeared through the doors into intensive care.

Pat's eyes gleamed triumphantly as she sat on the chair André had indicated.

Mortified, Claire followed André to Philippe's bedside. The small inert figure lay fighting for his life, and Claire's spirits reached their lowest ebb. She looked across at the tall figure of the surgeon, but he seemed not to notice her.

The Sister in charge of intensive care, noticing Claire's distress, said kindly, 'There's nothing more you can do here Nurse Baxter. We'll notify you of any change in Philippe's condition.'

'Thank you,' Claire murmured, blinking back the tears. She walked hurriedly towards the doors and out into the corridor. A faint waft of perfume assailed her nostrils, but she refused to look at Pat Johnson.

On she went . . . along the endless corridor, tormented by her seething emotions. She had lost them both—first Philippe, now André. Blindly she went out of the hospital and down the front steps. Henri came towards her.

'Mademoiselle . . . why, mademoiselle, let me help you.' He took her arm and led her towards the car where she sank on to the back seat, sobbing uncontrollably.

'How is Philippe?' asked Henri anxiously.

'I don't know. It's too soon to say. He's in intensive care.'

'Mademoiselle must be very tired. I'll take you back to Arcachon,' he said soothingly.

'Thank you, Henri.' She took a deep breath and dried her tears.

'Do you think we should wait for Dr Dubois?' he asked.

'No, I don't think we should,' she said firmly.

Henri let in the clutch and the car shot forward, through the streets of Bordeaux, and out along the road to Arcachon.

As she stepped out of the car, Madame Thiret came to meet her. 'How is he?' she asked nervously.

'We shall have to wait and see,' replied Claire truthfully. 'The operation was a success, but it all depends on his post-operative progress now.'

She went into the house and up to her room. It was still the same room, but somehow she didn't feel she belonged any more.

The telephone shrilled downstairs. She found herself hoping against hope that it would be for her, but Madame Thiret answered it and did not call her.

Later, as she tried to eat some supper, Madame Thiret said, 'Monsieur André called to say he will not be home tonight.'

Claire nodded listlessly. She pleaded a headache, and excused herself early. Somehow she got through the long dark hours of the night, until the first rays of the sun announced the new day. She was starting to dress, planning to take a walk along the shore, when the phone rang. Quickly she threw on a housecoat and ran along the landing, but Madame Thiret had reached it before her.

'Oh I'm so glad, I'll tell her,' she said as she put the phone down.

Raising her eyes the old lady saw Claire standing on the stairs. 'Ah, there you are my dear. I thought you would still be asleep. That was Monsieur André. He says Philippe is out of danger.'

A flood of relief swept over her, but at the same time it was tinged with sadness. Suddenly she shivered and pulled her housecoat round her.

'Are you cold, my dear?' asked Madame Thiret anxiously. 'Come and have some coffee. I've just made some.'

Claire followed the old lady into the kitchen and they sat by the stove drinking the strong, hot coffee.

'Are you ill, child?' asked Madame Thiret as she watched Claire.

'No, but I want to go away from here,' she said quietly.

Madame Thiret stared at her in disbelief. 'You

can't mean that, I thought you were so happy here.'

'I was, but . . . it's all changed . . . I don't think I'm needed any more.' It came out in a torrent of words.

The old lady's eyes widened. 'What are you saying child? Of course you are needed.'

'No, I'm not,' said Claire sadly. 'Marie is looking after Simone, and when Philippe comes out of hospital, Pat Johnson will be here to look after him. I want to go back to Paris. Do you think Henri will run me to the airport at Bordeaux?'

'Mademoiselle!' the old lady cried. 'Have you taken leave of your senses?'

But Claire was already half-way up the stairs. Dressing quickly, she flung her things hastily into her suitcase and went out to the car. Henri was leaning against it, enjoying a quiet, early morning smoke. He looked up, in surprise, as Claire approached carrying her suitcase.

'I have to go back to Paris,' she said briefly. 'Will you take me to the airport?'

'Yes, of course, mademoiselle.' He stubbed out his cigarette and took hold of her case.

'Mademoiselle!' Madame Thiret's voice called her from the steps. Claire turned.

'You are making a big mistake you know,' she said.

Claire reached out and grasped the old lady's hands. 'I can't stay now,' she said. 'Thank you for all your kindness. I shall never forget you.' She turned and got into the car.

CHAPTER TEN

As THE car sped along the motorway towards the airport, a sense of calm descended upon her with her new-found determination. She had been right to make this decision. It was obvious who André preferred, if she stayed on here, he would keep her on a piece of string until Pat finally agreed to marry him. She had to make the break now before she got hurt any more.

'Do you have a reservation, mademoiselle?' Henri was saying over his shoulder.

'Er . . . no . . . I'm hoping the plane won't be full.'

'If you don't mind me saying so, mademoiselle, I think you're being a bit optimistic. These internal flights are usually booked solid during the week, with businessmen.'

'Well I'll take the train, then,' she replied, amazed at the inner strength she had suddenly found.

'As you wish, mademoiselle.' Henri shrugged his shoulders and continued to drive furiously along the motorway.

As he pulled up in front of the airport, Claire started to gather her things together—passport, money, make-up, it was all there in her shabby old handbag.

'Thank you, Henri,' she said, as he lifted her suitcase out of the boot and handed it to her.

'I'll wait here for a while,' said Henri.

'Oh, that won't be necessary,' she said quickly.

'It might,' he said, with a wry grin. 'If you can't get a flight, come back and I'll drive you to the station.'

'You're very kind,' she said.

'*A votre service*, mademoiselle,' he smiled, pushing his peaked chauffeur's cap to the back of his head, and pulling out his cigarettes as he prepared to wait.

Claire went into the airport reception area and found the Air France desk.

'Mademoiselle?' said the friendly *hôtesse d'acceuil*.

'I'd like a flight to Paris this morning,' said Claire decisively.

'I'm sorry mademoiselle. We are fully booked until this evening,' was the polite reply.

Claire's spirits fell and with them went some of her new-found resolution.

'But I have to get away today,' she muttered, half to herself.

'Mademoiselle could try the railway station,' suggested the hostess kindly, sensing that Claire was going through some sort of traumatic experience.

'Thank you, yes I'll do that.' Claire turned away and picked up her luggage.

Henri smiled knowingly as she returned dejectedly to the car. He picked up her case and put it in the boot.

'The station?' he asked.

Claire nodded and climbed into the car. Henri drove through the streets of Bordeaux, weaving expertly in and out of the traffic, along the quayside with the huge ocean-going vessels moored alongside, and pulled up in front of the station. This time it was Claire who said, meekly,

'Will you wait, Henri?'

'*Bien sûr*,' mademoiselle,' he said with a grin. 'Leave your things here till you've bought your ticket. I'll bring them over to you.'

She smiled and went over to the booking office. Henri watched her taking her purse out of her bag, and gathered that this time she was successful. He picked up the bags and carried them to her.

'Oh thanks, Henri. I'm so lucky . . . the train leaves in ten minutes,' she said breathlessly, pushing her purse back into her bag.

'This way, mademoiselle. I think I'd better see you on to the train.'

Claire followed the reassuring figure of the chauffeur through the station. She showed her ticket at the platform barrier, and Henri poured out a torrent of voluble, colloquial French, which seemed to satisfy the ticket collector, for he gave a smile and waved Henri through.

She climbed into a compartment and Henri followed with the luggage.

'*Eh bien*, take care of yourself mademoiselle,'

said Henri. He placed the luggage on the rack, and prepared to leave. 'I don't know why you're going,' he added, 'But I hope we'll meet again.'

'I hope so too Henri,' said Claire. On impulse she reached up and kissed him lightly on the cheek. He looked surprised but pleased. '*Au revoir*, Henri, and thank you,' she said.

'*Au revoir*, mademoiselle,' he said, getting down from the train. '*Bon voyage*.' He waved his hand and was gone.

A feeling of utter loneliness fell upon her as the familiar figure went out of sight. She reminded herself once again that this was the only possible course of action. She thought of little Philippe, lying in his hospital bed. How she would miss him! But he's out of danger now, she comforted herself, and when he comes out of hospital he will be well-cared for . . . And Simone, I'll miss her too, but Marie will look after her. The train started to move slowly out of the station and Claire watched as the scene changed from streets to vineyards, and then to green rolling countryside. She leaned her head back against the seat and closed her eyes. The rhythmic movement of the train lulled her to sleep.

When she awoke she saw that the soft green countryside had given way to the harsher landscape of the north. She stared out of the window as the train hurtled relentlessly towards Paris.

No turning back now, she told herself. The die is cast.

As the train reached the outskirts of Paris, a thin

drizzle started to pour from the grey skies, directly reflecting Claire's mood. She struggled to get her case down from the rack as the train pulled into the station.

The long spell of hot weather had broken, and she felt cold as she walked along the platform dressed only in a cotton dress and a thin jacket. She stood outside the station waiting for a taxi.

Because of the rain, a long queue had formed and Claire stood at the end of it. Several taxis arrived and went, but the queue didn't seem to get any shorter. The covered waiting area stopped short just in front of Claire and by the time she had moved under its protection, she was wet through and feeling thoroughly miserable.

The man in front of Claire lit up a cigarette and the strong acrid fumes enveloped her. She turned away and started to cough.

'*Excusez-moi*, mademoiselle.' The man turned round and leered at her. 'Mademoiselle is alone?' he asked hopefully, in French. 'Perhaps we can share a taxi together?'

'I don't think so,' said Claire firmly in English as she stared fixedly out across the rain-sodden road.

It was half an hour before she reached the head of the queue and climbed into a taxi. Wet and cold, she gave the driver the Flaments' address. He drove quickly through the wet streets and deposited her, with her luggage, outside the apartment. The rain poured down upon her as she struggled off the pavement and up the steps to the foyer. She was shivering with cold as she got into the lift. She began to wonder if Madame Thiret had already phoned. I'll try and make myself presentable, she thought, before I go in to see Hélène.

The lift stopped at the penthouse suite and Claire went out through the doors. The familiar luxury of the soft carpets comforted her soaking feet. Her long wet hair was now dripping over her shoulders, she hurried down the corridor, hoping to reach the haven of her room before anyone saw her. She opened the door and hurried in.

There was someone standing by the window. At first she thought she must be dreaming. With long easy strides he crossed the room and took her in his arms.

'André!' she gasped in disbelief. 'What are you doing here?'

'Oh you silly child,' he said, laughing with relief. 'What do you think I'm doing here?'

'I . . . I . . . don't know,' she stammered.

'I flew here as soon as Madame Thiret phoned me. How could I possibly let you go,' he said, holding her so close that she could feel his heart beating.

'But what about Pat?' she murmured.

He pulled away and held her at arms' length. 'What about Pat?' he asked gently.

'She told me you had asked her to marry you.'

His face clouded over. 'I thought something like this might happen. Do you remember I said she was a complicated person? I also said you mustn't believe everything you heard. Of course I didn't ask her to marry me. She was so unreliable, my only concern was that she would care for the children properly—especially Philippe. This was why I spent so much time in Arcachon last year, and people jumped to the wrong conclusions.'

'But why did she leave?' asked Claire.

'I made it clear that she didn't interest me in the slightest, so when she met someone who *was* interested, she went away with him. That's all over now, which is why she's back in Arcachon, to see what she can find.'

'But why did you go to have a drink with her, that day when we had been sailing?' asked Claire, still perplexed.

'I went to tell her to stop spreading false rumours about us. She said she would, but apparently she has had some sort of nervous breakdown, since her boyfriend left her. She feels terribly insecure—in fact, I think she's now mentally unstable. I've advised her to see a psychiatrist. But my darling— you're shivering with cold— you're wet through! How thoughtless of me to keep you standing here like this. I was just so relieved to see you.'

'I must look a terrible mess,' said Claire, putting a hand up to her straggling hair.

'You look wonderful,' he breathed, kissing her tenderly on the lips. Then briskly he took her hand and led her over to the bathroom. 'Off with your wet things,' he ordered, as he turned on the shower.

She hesitated shyly, as he started to remove her sodden garments. Smiling lovingly, he took her in his arms. Above the noise of the cascading water he said,

'Claire, darling, will you marry me?'

'What did you say?' Claire's eyes were wide in amazement.

'I said, will you marry me,' he shouted.

'That's what I thought you said only . . .' she paused, 'I didn't think you were the marrying kind.'

'I'm not,' he laughed. 'But I shall have to make an exception just this once in my life—please don't keep me waiting for an answer—will you marry me?'

'Yes, oh, yes,' she murmured, as his parted lips closed over hers, sealing their love forever.

Some time later as she patted herself dry with the soft towels he said, 'Oh, by the way, I forgot to give this back to you.' In his hand lay her grandmother's silver comb. 'I promised myself I would keep it with me until you agreed to marry me. It's been in my pocket ever since I removed it from your hair, to remind me of you.'

Claire took the silver comb.

'But don't put your hair up just now,' he pleaded. 'It makes you so inaccessible.'

She moved into his arms again as he covered her hair with kisses.

'My darling little kitten,' he whispered. 'You've no idea how I wanted you that day, when I took you back to my apartment—but I didn't know if it was just the wine that was making you so responsive. I had to be sure you wouldn't regret it afterwards—especially as I thought you were still in love with Robert.'

'André, I was never in love with Robert . . .' she started to say, but he silenced her with a kiss.

Then, gently cupping her face in his hands, he murmured, 'It doesn't matter now, my darling. As you say in England, it's all water under the bridge. Tomorrow we must fly back to Arcachon to see Philippe. You will come with me won't you? I can't bear to let you out of my sight.'

'Of course I'll come. I'd follow you to the ends of the earth,' she whispered.

'But we still have tonight in Paris,' he murmured gently.

'Yes, we still have tonight . . .'

Doctor Nurse Romances

Amongst the intense emotional pressures of modern medical life, doctors and nurses often find romance. Read about their lives and loves in the other three Doctor Nurse titles available this month.

THE RETURN OF DR BORIS
by Lisa Cooper

'I have no intention of joining the harem,' Nurse Hollie Clinton declares when she hears how the charming Dr Boris is worshipped by the staff at Beattie's. But in spite of all her protestations she seems to be drawn magnetically towards the temperamental anaesthetist.

DOCTOR IN NEW GUINEA
by Dana James

'How can I possibly take someone like you into the dangers of a tropical forest,' Dr Nicholas Calder tells Maren Harvey when she joins him in Papua New Guinea. Though the instant antagonism between them is undeniable, Maren refuses to be deterred. Dr Calder has met his match...

ROSES FOR CHRISTMAS
by Betty Neels

Eleanor had been a little girl when she last saw Fulk van Hensum and vowed to hate him forever. When chance throws them together twenty years later she is a trained nurse and he is an eminent consultant. But her feelings towards the arrogant Dutchman have not changed... or have they?

Mills & Boon

the rose of romance